WED TO THE ALIEN WARLORD

ACCIDENTAL ALIEN BRIDES

JANUARY BELL

Wed To The Alien Warlord by January Bell

Published by January Bell

www.januarybellromance.com

Copyright © 2022 January Bell

Cover by Natasha Snow

Edited by Belle Manuel

Illustrations by Lucielart on Instagram

❀ Created with Vellum

CHAPTER
ONE

NIKI

THE THING they don't tell you in training, in the endless exercises, in the years of *yes, sirs* and *no, sirs*, is that you *never* feel ready for first contact, not really. At least, I certainly don't. I blow out a breath, inhale again, and hold it. Rinse and repeat.

"Five minutes. Landing gear deployed," an automated voice says overhead.

I want to move, to roll my neck, to do anything but sit here, strapped in. My palms sweat, but I don't dare wipe them off. My crew is watching me.

It's not my first mission, it's not even my tenth, but it doesn't matter.

It's the first time humans have been allowed in Suevan space, and everything is riding on this mission. Earth's hopes are with us. I inhale again, trying to calm my pounding heart. We pull this diplomatic mission off, and we've got an interplanetary defense system that will stave off any more alien incursions.

Humans might not survive the next one. Especially if it's like the last. My mind swirls, bile rising as an image of grey-skinned aliens tears through it, smoke churning through the streets, the screams of the survivors still ringing in my ears.

"Three minutes. Brace for impact." The automated words cut through the decades-old memory, and I inhale, pushing it down.

The ship likely won't do more than bounce a handful of times, but I grip the overhead roll bars out of habit. The safety netting stretches against my chest. I'm not going anywhere.

"This ship's such a fuckin' drama queen," Bex says, rolling her eyes. "All right, Captain Jacks?"

"Don't bother her," Gen says, half her lips curling up in a cocky smile. "Can't you see she's trying not to have a panic attack?"

Gen's our weapons specialist, and my best friend, and I probably let her get away with more than I should, even for second in command. She's like a gun that's always cocked, safety off. Probably not the best choice to take into potentially hostile space, but this isn't a normal mission. Not by a long shot.

"Insubordination," I say in reflex, but smile nonetheless. A light laugh goes up from my crew of seven, breaking some of the ice. I might let a little too much insubordination fly with this group.

We've been in space long enough that a lot of the shine of my superior officer status wore off a few months ago. We're a small team anyway, and we work well together. Once we're back planetside, though, I suspect the informality will fall away.

Not only are we the first humans allowed in Suevan space, but we're also the first female-only mission in Earth Federation history. No pressure. Our alien hosts insisted on it, and considering what's on the line for Earth, the Federation was only too happy to oblige.

Not that we saw any of that communication, and the little we did was redacted so thoroughly it wasn't even readable.

The ship rocks as it hits a thin atmospheric layer. I grit my teeth, but Gen's grin only grows more feral.

All I've got to go on is what the Federation crammed down our throats during our mission briefing.

From what little we know of the Suevans, they're a warlike race, seemingly barbaric, mostly living pastorally in small settlements throughout their jungle planet. Very traditional. At first look, they seem almost primitive… until you see their warships. Until you see the footage of them in action. Their weapons and knowledge are centuries ahead of where we are on Earth, and if we want Earth to stay free of some of the nastier alien civilizations out there, we need to catch up.

Fast.

"Landing initiated," the ship chimes.

My ears pop for a fourth time, and we all raise up on our toes, letting the impact roll through loose knees and hips, the kinetically charged safety webbing absorbing any additional energy. We're landing in one of the numerous Suevan settlements, and we need to be ready to hit the ground running. We don't have time for landing sickness, so I've got my crew standing, strapped in and kitted out. Just in case.

"Get ready." I grin, adrenaline starting to pump through me, excitement at finally being here after so long in space. Faster than we thought possible, though, thanks to the tech the Suevans have already shared with us through their simple communications.

Bex smirks at me, pointing at the ridiculous 'monster fucker' sticker on her helmet. I bite my cheeks to keep from laughing. At least she's excited about meeting the aliens.

"No extracurricular activity," I tell her.

"What if I told you I had a whole bucket of candy under my bunk for you to look the other way?" Bex bats her eyelashes, and I snort.

"I'd confiscate your candy and write you up anyway." Jesus. Now all I can think about is my own candy stash, which will be waiting for me when we get back to the ship tonight.

I will have fucking earned it.

"Don't forget the briefing." Our xenobiologist, Carmen, pats her curly hair, her eyes wide. "They've written that they're willing to embed the translators for us, but we have to partake in the welcoming ceremony. They consider their spoken language sacred, so this is a really—"

"Big deal," the rest of the crew says in unison.

"We know, Carmen," Gen says, grinning at her. "We'll be on our best behavior."

"It's *you* she's worried about," I tell her.

"This face?" Gen flutters her eyelashes. "They can't get mad at me."

Bex snorts. "The fucking ridiculous thing is she's right. They never see Gen coming."

Gen's so gorgeous that if she wasn't hilarious and tough and loyal, it might make me sick.

The rest of the crew's silent, but everyone's eyes are alert, their body posture signaling that they're ready.

"First contact, ladies. This is their show. We are here to do a job. We follow their lead, we play nice, we get the tech, we go home. We don't have language capabilities, so we will be at a disadvantage until they decide to gift us with their translators. Assume they know what we're saying, and don't fuck up by saying something stupid. The last thing we need is an intergalactic incident."

"Aye-aye, Captain." They say it at once, with not a hint of irony.

"Ship is secured and ready for departure. Alien lifeforms approaching," the ship says.

"Release restraints," I tell the ship, and they immediately zip back, releasing our bodies. Several crew stagger, then right themselves.

"Bex, lock it down," I continue. "We're here to play nice, but there's no reason to make it easy for them to slip something on board we don't want." With their level of equipment, it's all too likely we won't have a clue if they do, but taking precautions is better than doing nothing at all.

Bex launches herself at a nearby terminal, her fingers flying over the key screens. The nervous energy is palpable as everyone removes their helmets, Carmen's hair fanning about her like cotton candy. Mmm, sugar.

I should have put some candy in my pockets. For safe keeping.

"We ready?" I ask, knowing it's the last time we'll be able to speak freely until we're spaceside again, hopefully sooner than later. Then I can get my promotion, some glory, and secure Earth's future. No biggie.

"Ready," they chorus.

"Open doors," I tell the ship. "Let's say hello, shall we?"

I fix my best smile to my face, and the loading dock door hisses open, descending into a ramp.

Nothing I studied could have prepared me for this.

"Holy shit," someone says, probably Bex. Another whistles in appreciation. We've landed in a clear area, but dense, verdant jungle crowds all around us. That's not the cause for their unprofessional but warranted exclamations, though.

This place is incredible.

Humidity blasts through the door, viscous fingers of steam that curl across my face. Sweat begins sliding between my breasts, but I stand straight, leading my crew down the ramp and onto Suevan ground.

The *first* humans on Suevan ground.

My heart flutters a little. This is easily the biggest mission of my career, and for a second, I'm giddy with it. I've dedicated my entire life to the Earth Federation, spent so many nights lonely and tired, but it's all worth it now.

They've finally found me fit to lead an entire mission.

Lights dance above the ground, shedding warm light into the dusky evening. Massive trees cage in the clearing, and more bobbing lanterns float around them, illuminating what appears to be a city carved into the trunks of the trees themselves.

The Suevan welcoming committee approaches, and I instantly go on high alert. My heart rate picks up, hammering against my chest. We knew they were huge, we've gone over what we know of them over and over again in Carmen and our intel officer's daily briefings, but it's one thing to see the Suevans in vids and an entirely different thing to have the over seven foot aliens gliding up to you in real life.

Thank goodness we at least had the vids, our ability to tap into alien comms streams thanks to tech leftover from the Roth invasion of Earth over a decade ago, the invasion that completely changed the course of Earth's future.

I swallow hard, forcing myself to remain calm. That ability, at least, is thanks to the years of training the Federation's put me through.

Several of my crew suck in noisy breaths, shifting uneasily behind me.

Daunting even from a distance, the huge lizard people are a meld of recognizable human features too. Talons jut from human-like five fingered hands and larger than human feet. Fangs flicker in the overhead lights, pressing against mouths that are otherwise like ours. A huge tail sweeps from the back of each Suevan, thick and flexible.

But it's their skin that truly sets them apart: glossy scales in different shades of green that fade to orange and creamy yellow on their exposed chests and stomachs.

"Do you think they have Crossfit here?" Gen asks, and Bex laughs quietly.

I shoot her a warning glance, but she's right. The Suevans are packed with hard muscle, muscle that's all too on display with their lack of clothing, other than the pants they wear. Their bodies look built for this planet... and for war.

My own clothes are stifling in the sticky heat, and I fight the urge to adjust them, the urge to show any discomfort at all, in front of these primal predators.

"Oh, shit," Gen says breathily, and I zero in on the cause of her discomfort.

These aren't just any Suevans.

I recognize at least three immediately, from the few vids we have of them in battle. Though the footage we've studied over and over is garbled, there's no mistaking the ragged scar knifing down the lead alien's face. It starts at the top of his head, cuts down the side of his face, barely missing his eye.

Draz of Edrobaz, First Warlord and right hand of the monarchy. It's about all we know about him, thanks to the communiques they sent to Earth. That, and that this alien, Draz, is a butcher. I repress a shudder as I recall what those huge arms are capable of, what his hands did on the field of battle as he protected a small Suevan settlement on a nearby moon. His scales are a dark, mossy green which fade to a warm yellow across the hard ridge of his pecs and abdomen, muscled far beyond what any human would be capable of achieving. A body spent in a lifetime of honing it into a weapon.

He is dangerous.

And I can't look away. When his gaze skates over me, his diamond-shaped pupils dilate, and his eyes widen slightly. I lift my chin, refusing to show anything but strength. Some animal sense in me screams to do otherwise would endanger my whole crew.

Behind me, Gen tenses, her hand brushing my forearm.

"Stand down," I mutter. We have to play by their rules. If they wanted us dead, they would have shot us down in space. They would have closed the temporary wormhole they set up on the edge of Earth designated space as we went through.

They don't want us dead. I inhale, stiffening my shoulders. Now I just have to figure what, exactly, they *do* want.

Piece of cake.

The approaching Suevan males slow, and dread settles deep

in my belly. Strange music cues, and First Warlord Draz flicks his long, powerful tail in time to it. Right. Warlords in relaxation mode. Sure.

I clear my throat, trying to be calm and collected. "Thank you for welcoming us to your beautiful planet," I manage. "We hope to learn much of your culture and take your teachings back to Earth with us." *And your tech.*

Carmen insisted I make some kind of opening remark, that they likely have some sort of translator implant for human languages. But Draz frowns, and I wonder if I've said something culturally offensive.

He rumbles something, their language guttural and full of a strange throaty hissing, and the huge reptilian males behind him exchange glances.

"Right," I say, trying to gauge what the hell is happening here, and how I've misstepped.

We don't have a lot of information to work with regarding their people, and frankly, Federation top brass seemed beyond surprised that the Suevans even agreed to entertain our negotiations, considering how closed off they are. They intervene in few galactic skirmishes, mostly to defend their territories and settlements in the surrounding moons and small planets, where they mix with other alien species. It's the only way we found out about their weapons and defense capabilities; the videos of their fighters are some of the most streamed on Earth.

And here those fighters are, in the flesh, a hair's breadth from us.

Draz says something else, motioning for us to follow. That particular gesture, at least, seems universal. I step forward, and his lip curls, showing a hint of fang. He offers an arm to me, and I straighten my back, trying to radiate a confidence I do not feel in the slightest.

I swallow hard and move to slip my arm into his.

But when I reach for it, I realize I've misread his body language. Which of course I did, he's an alien. The scarred warlord doesn't let me take his elbow at all; instead, he wraps his arm around my waist. I freeze, staring up at him in shock. His hand is warm and wide, and altogether too comfortable along the curve of my hip.

I should absolutely *not* like the way his hand feels there.

I squirm. There's no protocol for this. Maybe they're a touchy-feely species. Never would I have guessed it, but I'm not the xenobiologist—I'm the captain.

He leans his head down, muttering something that sends a shiver down my spine. I can't shake the feeling that I'm in way, way over my head. But there's nothing for it now, and I let him pull me along to where more Suevans gather, dancing and feasting.

I chance irritating him and glance back at the rest of my crew, hoping they're managing.

All seven are likewise being led to the welcoming ceremony, a huge Suevan male wrapped around each. Except Gen, who glares at the one next to her like she's daring him to try. I briefly squeeze my eyes shut. *God, I hope she doesn't punch him.*

Suddenly, I have a really, really bad feeling about this.

CHAPTER
TWO

DRAZ

THE HUMAN FEMALES are more than any of us had hoped. Surprise still zings through me as I gaze at her strange green and gold flecked eyes. The first off their primitive ship, the captain defied any and all expectations I had for the small females. Her authority struck a chord with me, as did the way the rest of the females responded to it. This one knows what it is to lead.

She will make a fine mate.

Prince Kanuz even seems pleased with his choice—a sunny-haired human with pleasing, symmetrical features, though she seems ill-tempered to me.

I can hardly breathe as I glance at the woman next to me. Tiny brown dots scatter across her narrow nose and high cheeks, her flesh soft and warm under my hands, so different from my own hard skin. Will she find my tough scaled hide disturbing? If she does, she does not show it.

I want her to find me as pleasing as I find her.

I did not expect to feel so… strongly.

In fact, I expected to do what I have always done for the Suevan people. My duty.

But now, I look at the woman I've hand-picked to mate and bed, and I cannot help a surge of reckless anticipation. I squash it down, piling a plate high with the choicest Suevan delicacies. The gilded dish settles heavily on the long, carved table, and a floating light drifts by, illuminating her ethereal, captivating features.

I bow my head towards her, wanting to soak her in, to live in this moment.

The captain leans further away from me. She makes a small, musical noise as she worms out of my grasp.

My translator provides the interpretation of her strange sounds. "I am going to sit over here."

"Next to me," I respond. When she stares up at me with those striking eyes, I pat the seat, showing her where I want her to sit.

They cannot implant the translator in her soon enough. I want to be able to converse with this female. The music picks up in tempo, the perzo drum and ceph flutes signifying the beginning of the ritual. All around me, couples are hand feeding each other, older, mated Suevan couples renewing their bonds. There are no new couples. There have not been any new mates in years. There are no females to have them with.

A silver-haired male places a morsel in his mate's mouth, and she smiles, chewing slowly, his hand brushing her mouth.

Like I soon will to the female human sitting beside me.

My cock grows painfully hard at the thought, the forceful thrust of desire shocking through me. Eager to begin, I pick out a choice cube of quarn and push it at her face. Her green eyes widen, and she jerks away from me.

"Eat," I tell her. "You will enjoy this. I will enjoy this. Then we will enjoy each other."

Her strange human nose wrinkles at my speech.

"What do you think you're doing?" a voice screeches. A commotion rises behind where I am trying to soothe my new female, and she and I both turn at once. Her expression is thunderous, her mouth a thin line.

The fair-haired pretty one slaps a piece of food from Prince Kanuz's hands, and the spiced norlamiz goes flying.

"First Officer Durand," my new mate spits the words, clearly furious at her behavior. "You are to partake in the welcoming ceremony."

Welcoming ceremony? Perhaps the translator is incorrect. Surely she meant the mating ritual. I make a mental note to have our tech update the human grammar later.

Captain Jacks clears her throat, making a pitiful coughing sound, and I crane my head down, examining her for illness. I do not want my chosen mate to be ill, and unanticipated worry threads through me.

"This is the part where you feed us? To welcome us?" Her eyes narrow meaningfully, and then she fixes me with a hard stare.

A thrill goes through me.

My little human female wants to lead by example.

All of her crew stares at us now, their many-hued eyes wide and curious. Many of the Suevan watch, too, interested in the drama the new members of our society present. Carefully, I put the quarn down, trading it for the tastiest piece of jex meat, roasted and spiced until it's tender and smokey.

I step closer, my tail flicking madly, the drums beating ever faster. A bead of sweat drips from my female's neck, dropping into the raised mounds of her ample chest. I lick my lips. What will it be like to feel them? To chase that sweat with my tongue and watch the look of disapproval melt from her face, replaced by her moans of desire?

First, the ritual. I hold the jex out to her, and her delicate, rounded nostrils, so different from mine, flare as the meat approaches her lush mouth. When a smooth pink tongue darts out, a small groan erupts from me, and her eyes dart up, away from the meat. My fingertips brush the curve of her lip as I place the jex in her mouth, careful to keep my talons from shredding her fragile flesh.

The sight of her lips closing over the jex I hunted yesterday in preparation for this ceremony, the sign of her accepting our mating, is more arousing than anything I've ever seen in my life.

I have never been so hard in all my days.

A cheer goes up from the crowd, and we turn back to the yellow-haired woman, who frowns, but accepts Prince Kanuz's morsel. Her nose wrinkles as she chews, but she swallows it, accepting him as her mate. I don't bother watching the rest of the females, too taken with the delicate creature next to me to care.

"You must feed me now, little human." I nudge her hand towards the food, so that she understands.

She hesitates, a flicker of concern flashing over her expressive face, before blowing out a breath and selecting a good hunk of jex. When she tilts her chin up, her eyes filled with grim determination, I pause. That is not the expression I would like to see on my mate's face, not during our ritual. Not ever, when approaching me.

But her lips turn up at the corners, and a playful light shines in her expressive eyes.

"When in Rome, right?" she mutters quietly, depositing the jex on my tongue with efficient precision.

The delicious taste, usually my favorite, tastes like ash in my mouth.

The only thing I care about tasting now is sitting beside me.

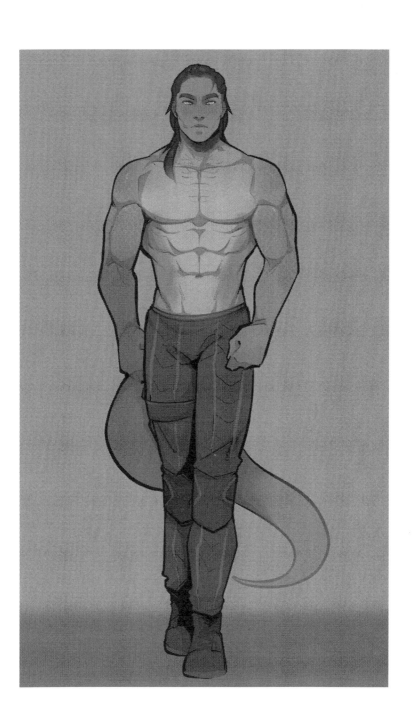

CHAPTER
THREE

NIKI

RELIEF SHOOTS THROUGH ME. The food is good, especially delicious after eating prepackaged space meals, and even though being the focus of all the hulking alien's attention is slightly concerning, he's been very respectful and polite.

He can clearly understand the words I'm saying, and tries to communicate back, despite the fact I have no idea what he's saying. I hope my crew are remembering my order not to say anything stupid. A quick check shows they're relaxing, too, all except Gen, who never relaxes, and our intel officer, Michelle, who's analytical gaze misses nothing. Her face is uncharacteristically pale. She mostly ignores the alien sitting next to her, only doing the bare minimum of politeness.

Hmm. I'll have to ask what it is she's figured out as soon as this welcoming ceremony is over. Maybe it will help us get out of here quicker.

Draz holds up a pitcher of some kind of sparkling liquid, pouring it into a mug. When he pushes it at me, I try to take it from him.

He grins at me again, those sharp fangs flashing, and brushes my hands away.

Right. This again. Must be some kind of guest ritual—we offer you bread and water or whatever else, and that signifies some kind of secure place in their household while visiting. Makes sense, and I know several human cultures have similar principles.

He holds the cup up again, saying something guttural in a low voice, and I try to smile back at him.

This is weird. I can't put my finger on what it is, but something about this entire shebang is completely and utterly off. There have been no welcoming speeches. No group activities. We've all been separated, paired up with a Suevan warlord apiece.

Though, perhaps the speeches will come after we've accepted their bread and salt or whatever, and they decide were worthy enough to bestow their sacred translator tech upon us.

So I let Draz of Edrobaz, the scarred warlord capable of tearing a spine out of his enemies, press the cup to my lips. I try not to think too hard about the spine thing as I take a sip.

It's cool and refreshing, the taste somewhere between lemon and cucumber, and it's welcome in the heat and humidity of the jungle.

He says something to me again, and I jerk back as he brushes his knuckles against my cheek.

"That's a little too familiar, buddy," the words snap out of me, surprising me. I eye the cup, wondering at the contents. Alcohol? Drugs? I feel… fizzier than I should. Lighter.

He makes a harsh barking sound, and I rear back, on guard, until I realize he's laughing. He retracts his hand though, and it clenches into a fist on the table as he continues to talk.

He stands suddenly, holding his elbow out like he did when he escorted me from our ship, which still sits on one side of the clearing, the lights of whatever the strange floating lanterns are reflecting off the many silver solar panels. I blink, and a slight dizzy sensation washes over me.

The drums pick up, and I stand, letting Draz, the most fearsome Suevan warlord, tug me towards where the Suevans dance.

"I am not a good dancer," I tell him.

He shrugs, muttering a harsh string of syllables I don't have a chance of understanding. The rest of my crew are filing onto the polished surface, too, each led by the male that escorted them from our ship.

Draz grabs my hand, and I try to swallow down my instinct that screams something is wrong.

The Federation made it quite clear that if we were to succeed at this mission, at helping defend Earth by shoring up our defenses, that we had to win the Suevans over.

If that means a little harmless dancing, so be it.

Unfortunately, whatever was in that lemon and cucumber tasting drink must have been alcohol, because the familiar buzz of it turns my limbs loose, and suddenly, I'm smiling and clapping, imitating the huge warlord's steps as best I can. Beside me, Bex is laughing, and even Gen has a slight foolish grin. Only Michelle stands still, her arms crossed on her chest, her face furious.

I need to check on her.

But the music is so good it seems to sweep me up in its embrace, my heart pounding in time to the intoxicating drums, and I push it away for a moment and just enjoy dancing.

CHAPTER
FOUR

DRAZ

MY LITTLE FEMALE sets me on fire. Unaccustomed though she is to our mating dance, her body moves sinuously, her soft curves enticing.

And she said she was a bad dancer.

I would watch her dance like this for me, this mating dance, every night. Though she is not Suevan, the genetic information her people sent proved beyond a shadow of a doubt their species is compatible with ours. Lust rides me hard at the thought. A low growl tears from my throat, and swish my tail, knocking it against the back of her knees and bringing her closer into me.

Her breath gusts against my chest, and her pleased expression fades, replaced by wariness at my proximity.

I do not understand it. She has accepted my gift of food and wine, and she has performed my dance in front of our people. She should be eager to come to me now.

No matter. Perhaps this shyness is a way of her people. The more I think on it, the more it makes sense. They cover their delicate skin with primitive fabrics. They must be a conservative species.

I growl again, wrapping my hand around her soft waist. I want to rip that fabric from her body and spend the rest of the night exploring it.

The music dies, and my female moves to step away from me, but I hold her tight.

A small noise of protest sounds from the fragile column of her throat, but I point to the Suevan medic circulating, a platter of translators held in front of him.

"He will give you this, and then, when I say how much I desire you, you will finally understand my need for you."

Her pretty eyes are round, and her throat bobs as she swallows. I watch the movement, fascinated by how fragile she is, that I can see the movement. Before I can think better of it, I run a finger down her throat, curious.

Instead of shying away this time, though, she watches me curiously, lips parted slightly.

Yes. This is good. *This* is more like it.

The medic hands a translator implant to Kanuz first, and everyone cheers as he takes it. The medic comes to me next, and I take the tech from him carefully. My woman watches with big eyes.

I motion for her to turn her head. Even her ears are insubstantial looking, thin veins visible along the incredibly soft shell of it.

"This will not hurt her?" I demand of the medic. I cannot imagine harm coming to this creature, would rather cut off my own hand than administer something to her that might mar her smooth flesh.

"No. We engineered it with the information her government sent. It will work. They'll be fine."

"It better," I snarl at him. The medic ducks his head in a sign of respect, scurrying away as he seems to remember who he is speaking to.

"I am going to put this in your ear now, sweet wife," I tell her. "He says it will not hurt." I touch my own ear, trying to show her what's going to happen.

Obediently, she tilts her head, allowing me access. Her thick brown braid slips over her neck, falling away down her back.

My cock strains against my pants. I yearn to claim her, to mark that smooth shoulder with my bite, and to make her fully mine. My mate.

I thought I would never have one, not after the virus that swept through our people devastated our female population.

And here she is.

Not Suevan, it is true, but perfect nonetheless. And to think, the southern separatists were against finding a way to interbreed with other species. Idiots.

I pinch the small part of her ear, and she goes still under my hands. I grit my teeth, trying to push down the thick wave of desire and concentrate on inserting the miniscule translator into the tiny opening of her ear canal.

It slips in, and she tenses under my hands. The device crawls along her inner ear until it slips from view. My mate makes a hissing noise, the sound slipping from her teeth, her eyes squeezed shut.

"She is in pain," I yell, anger burning through me. "My mate is in pain," I say. I am not the only one yelling for the medic however. Kanuz is near frantic, the yellow-haired human dropping to her knees.

Another human female screams, a garbled stream of words that my translator interprets as fecal matter and other foul words.

None of us are paying attention to anything other than the women we've mated to when their ship explodes, sending spirals of flame and heat into the dark Suevan night.

My mate's eyes go wide, her mouth open in a silent scream, showing off her tiny flat teeth, and then she melts into me, unconscious.

Everything in me screams to haul her away. I have to get her to safety.

"It's the separatists," Alvez screams at me, whipping his tail in a frenzy behind him. He hauls his own mate to his chest. "We were short-sighted. We should have shielded this place. We are too exposed here."

"Separate," I bark the order. "We lead them through the jungle, and we do not make it easy on them by staying together." I should have known they would try something like this. "Reconvene at Edrobaz," I shout over the chaos. "Protect the females, they are the future of our people."

"Do as he says." Prince Kanuz hauls the yellow-haired woman over one shoulder, her head lolling.

The Acriset tree, the bustling hub of this outpost, explodes a moment later, sending bark and shrapnel through the clearing. The rest of the couples, the older ones, scream as pieces of wood sail by them. One bleeds from a head wound, and her mate drags her to the safety of the woods, surrounded by the others, all ready to fight.

By the hand of Sueva, I am relieved I cleared the few families from it two mornings ago to prepare for tonight. The feast is ruined, our mating ritual luckily over before the separatists struck.

The tables and meal can be replaced, the ceph flutes remade, but the people cannot be. Our numbers are too thin as it is, and it cracks my heart to think the discontent among the southern Suevans is high enough to warrant such bloodshed.

My legs stretch as I break into a run, holding my beautiful female tight to my chest, swearing vengeance on the short-minded separatists attacking us.

I will make them pay.

CHAPTER
FIVE

NIKI

MY LIDS ARE TOO HEAVY. Something's crawling inside my ear, scratching so damn loudly I can hardly hear myself think. Every time I slap at it though, trying to dislodge whatever nasty's crawled inside, someone holds my wrist back.

I have weird dreams, too, of exploding ships and an attack on the Suevan city.

Attack on the Suevan city...

My eyelids fly open, and I sit up with a gasp, my heart racing a mile a minute. The knowledge that something has gone terribly, completely wrong, weighs heavy on me, and my adrenaline kicks into overdrive.

"Calm yourself," a deep, gravelly voice says.

I clap a hand over my ear, fishing for whatever has crawled inside. "Get it out, get it out," I say, deeply unsettled, but too woozy to do more than clutch at my head.

"It cannot come out, nor would I want to take it out," the same voice says.

A scarred, green face swims into view, and my eyes go wide.

Draz of Edrobaz. The night's events come rushing back to me, and I lay back down, my mouth dry and my head pounding.

The ship. Oh my God, the ship blew up. My crew.

"What happened?" I rasp, blinking up at the stars, twinkling in patches of deep black through the jungle canopy. Okay. We're in the jungle. Animal sounds rush at me, the startlingly loud chirp of insects, the calls of an alien creature that I can't place. A large white flower blooms in the night, a living moon suspended from a green vine. A fire crackles beside me, blinding me as I glance at it. "Is my team safe?"

"They were well last I saw," Draz says.

A cool rag swipes across my brow, and I turn my head. He's sponging my forehead off. The sides of his mouth curl up, showing a hint of fang. I swallow, because despite the scales, the green color, the flattened nose— he's almost handsome. Brutally so, his jaw too square and brow too strong to be human... but there's something undeniably attractive about him, all masculine power.

The packed-on muscle of his chest still on full display doesn't hurt, either.

What the fuck is going on?

"We split up to make it harder on the perpetrators. We will reconvene with your team at an agreed upon location up in the mountains."

"The perpetrators of what? Who are they?"

"There are separatists who do not approve of... the hard choices we have had to make." He says this carefully, unblinking, so still and alien that a shiver runs down my spine. "They blew up your ship."

"Okay," I say, trying to process. So that was real. The ship is gone. A wild laugh tears from my throat. "I guess I'm not getting my candy tonight."

"Can-dee?" The word sounds strange coming from his mouth, and I realize it must not have translated. He's repeating it in English.

"Sweets. I love sweets. Sugary, gummy, sweets." Fuck. And I'm not getting them. They're all gone. Blown to smithereens.

The ship is gone. My throat constricts. A luminescent green insect floats over the flower, drawn by its glow and delicate fragrance. The winged insect crawls along the petal, long proboscis darting from its mouth, surreal as it drinks from the—

Snap.

The petals slam shut around the glowing bug, and it makes a high pitched chirp that cuts off quickly.

My eyes go wide.

"Sweets," he repeats, and I swivel my head towards him. I can't shake the feeling that something has crawled into my ear, and I give my head a careful tilt, trying to loosen it.

"I am furious that the translator embed has affected you thusly, my wife."

I stare at him. The fire casts strange shadows across the planes of his face. Surely, I heard him wrong. I sit up slowly, smashing the palm of my hand against my ear.

"No," he hisses, circling my wrist with his talon-tipped fingers. "Do not hurt yourself, wife. Why would you do such a thing?"

The translator must be misfiring. It must be wrong.

"Why do you keep calling me that?" It comes out hoarse.

His thumb slides down my forearm. I jerk away from him.

"Because you just wed me. We are mated." A satisfied smirk punctuates this statement, and all air seems to leave my lungs.

It takes me a moment to get enough oxygen back to formulate a response.

"What do you mean we just wed?" Maybe these aliens have a different definition of the word. Maybe my translator is glitching.

"It means you're mine now, little human." There's a predatory hunger in his eyes.

I don't give him an inch. My throat's gone dry, my heart flipping in my chest, but he doesn't have to know that.

"Not according to any laws on Earth." I'm not entirely sure how I'm managing to form coherent sentences at this point.

That strange barking sound comes from him again, and I realize he's laughing again.

Did I think he was polite and respectful earlier? Anger curls through me.

"You are not on Earth." He smooths a strand of hair away from my face, the wet piece of cloth brushing against my temple. It's almost tender.

I grit my teeth. I have to be smart about this. I need to be diplomatic. Earth needs their tech. My people need it, if we want to stand a chance of maintaining our planetary independence.

"What troubles you, human wife?" His tail swishes, and his scaly forehead wrinkles.

"Call me that again and lose your favorite body part," I snarl.

A grin kicks up the side of his mouth.

"It will be your favorite body part, too. But if you prefer another name, I am only too happy to acquiesce, Captain Jacks." He's still smiling at me, like I've said something adorable.

I stare at him. Most men I know would take my threat for what it was: a promise to do severe bodily injury to their dick or balls, or if I felt generous, all three.

I'm still considering it when the truth snaps into place in my head. The heavily redacted comms. The oath we swore to do whatever it took to get the tech. The Federation's choice of an all-female team. Michelle's fearful, anxiety ridden expression at the ceremony.

The bottom of my stomach drops out.

CHAPTER
SIX

DRAZ

HER GREEN AND gold eyes close slowly, and I watch, fascinated, as her long eyelashes meet and part again. When they open fully, they're wide in disbelief, her mouth slightly parted.

How I long to feel that mouth against me.

"Did they know?" she croaks.

It is an odd question, and I cannot for the life of me figure out who or what she is talking about, so I wait for further information. An insect buzzes around my head, another victim for the pale petals of the jono flower behind me.

"Did Earth… Did my command know? The Federation. They knew you planned to wed us?"

The realization pierces me. I stumble back with the force of it. My sweet human female did not know she was marrying me. The Federation deceived us both.

She did not agree to it.

My fists clench at my sides, guilt sliding through me. Rage follows quickly on its heels, but I swallow it down, refusing to show her my anger. She does not need my anger.

She needs my protection. Now, more than ever.

She lets out a harsh laugh, and there is no humor in it. In fact, her eyes spark with water, and concern grows through me.

"You are producing liquid here," I point to my own eyes, everything in me screaming to comfort her. But I know if I move to touch her again, she will not be pleased.

I want to please her. I want to give her pleasure like she has ever known. My tail lashes furiously against the ground.

"No, I am not," she chokes out, then frowns at me, as though furious I have pointed out the liquid.

"You are," I tell her earnestly, real concern threading through me. "Is it a sickness?" I bend closer, trying to determine the cause.

She leans back, grabbing a fallen zitsu leaf, and brandishes it like a weapon at me. It might be threatening, were she not a head and a half smaller than me… and were it not for the fact the zitsu leaf flops around like a fish on a bank.

Instead, it is adorable.

I sink to my heels, studying her. Her smooth throat bobs, a motion I will never cease to be intrigued by. My hand goes to my own throat on reflex, and all I feel there is the hard armored plating of my scales. What must it be like to be so fragile?

I can think of one hundred things in this jungle that would be only too happy to make a meal out of my perfect wife.

"You are afraid," I say. It makes me sick. "What have I done to frighten you?"

"I am not afraid." She sticks her chin up, her eyes still watery. Every inch of her is defiance. "Answer the damn question. Did my command know that you planned to wed us at the welcoming ceremony?"

"Of course, they did. We did not expect our mates to be so beautiful," I say cautiously, half afraid she will hurt herself by smashing the zitsu leaf into the wrong part of my scaled hide. I must choose my words carefully.

She bares her small, blunt teeth, and growls—*growls!*—at me.

It is quite charming, and I can't help flashing my own fang in a smile back at her.

"Did they not tell you?"

"No," she grits out, and alarm rises in me as more water slips down her cheeks.

I do not say anything though, as she does not seem to enjoy talking about the water. So I stare at it, my gaze flicking from the water back to her eyes, where more water forms.

"Is it a sign of thirst?" I finally ask, unable to contain my concern.

She waves the zitsu leaf again. "It is a sign that I am royally, completely, absolutely furious."

Am I supposed to be afraid of the zitsu leaf? I am not sure, so I ignore it, watching my little mate sniffle miserably.

"With your command?" I ask. "You are angry with your command?"

The look she gives me tells me that she meant her threat about chopping off my balls, and I cup myself protectively.

"Right," I say.

I stalk away, feeding the small fire another branch, careful to keep the flames low enough that the separatists will have trouble finding us in the jungle.

"Why wouldn't they tell us? Why didn't they give us a choice?"

Ah. This is a refrain I am familiar with, and I open my mouth to answer her question about leadership and communication, then snap it closed with a shut.

I might be the First Warlord of Sueva, used to command, but I have no experience with her situation.

This is not a normal problem I have had with my warriors. I have ordered them to do things they were uncomfortable with in the name of conditioning, or things that were unpleasant that had to be done, but I never once ordered them to an alien planet to marry in exchange for weapons.

Anger wells for her, eclipsing my own need, as full as the heavy moon in the Suevan night sky.

"I am sure they would have found *someone* willing," she says, her voice trembling with rage.

Sadness washes away some of the anger, and I turn back to Niki. Her wide gaze fixes on the asteroid belt just visible through the jungle canopy.

She is not only angry that she was tricked by her command, the sneaky Earth Federation. Vile behavior.

But no. She also finds *me* displeasing.

A low growl rasps against my throat, and I flick my tail, immeasurably upset.

I turn away from her, facing the jono flower as it demolishes another insect, rather than see the hurt writ across her face.

True, we are very different from the soft hided males of their planet. It's clear from the snarled way she said someone, as though mating a Suevan is a disgusting proposition. A new problem to overcome.

It has been a long, long time since I had a female, and perhaps my scar mars my face, but I have never had any complaints, not on Sueva, nor on any of our settlements, with the few Suevan females left, and a few other species, as well.

"Do you not find my form pleasing, w—woman?" I almost say wife, but I do not want to set her off again, and change words at the last minute as I face her.

Stepping into the firelight, I hold myself still for her perusal. Well, perhaps I flex a little, but why shouldn't I? My muscles are proof of my status, my age, my reputation.

I can keep you safe, they say. *I am a fierce predator, and a fiercer protector.*

Her defiant gaze holds mine for a moment, and then slips down my scales, from my oversize shoulders, big even by Suevan warlord standards, to my abdomen. Lower still. I clear my throat. Maybe that is the problem. Maybe she thinks I will not fit.

"Do you worry that I will be too big for you?" I say, making my voice softer now.

A choked noise erupts from her. "What? Oh my *Jesus*." She buries her face in her hands.

"My name is Draz, not Jesus," I say. There's no translation that makes sense for that word, and it offers up a name and an image of a human with long facial hair. "I cannot grow much hair on my chin. It only grows on the top of my head. Is that the problem?"

Her eyes are huge in her face now, and a musical laugh trickles out of her. My eyes close at the noise. What a wondrous sound.

"No," she manages. "No, you are fine. You are nice looking. Very muscled." She shakes her head, as though she can't quite believe she's said that. "Draz, I need to know something right now."

"Anything." My name is like nectar from her lips. I want her to say it again.

"Will the other Suevans… the other warlords—" She bites her lip, clearly unwilling or too uncomfortable to continue speaking. I want to tug it from her little teeth. Blunt though they are, her pink lip turns white under the sustained pressure. "Will they force them?"

"What?"

"My crew. Will the other warlords—" She releases her lips, pinning me with an angry stare. "Will they force them to have sex?"

I recoil physically, her implication bringing shame to me and my people. "That is not done. That is a death sentence. Females are treasured. Valued." Horror spreads through me, bile rising in my throat. "What you suggest is the gravest of offenses."

She sags, relief turning her limbs loose.

My female truly believes Suevans would force her crew… Force *her*. No Suevan woman would ever even consider this, which means—

"This is done on Earth? Your males hurt your women?"

"It isn't sanctioned. It's illegal there, too," she spits out, crossing her arms. Defensively, I realize. She still thinks to defend the males of her species, even if they act abominably?

What a strange, proud creature. I blink slowly, my third eyelid closing and opening, as I ponder her.

As I ponder what to say, a steady patter of rain begins. Sueva herself is angry at my mate's people, and lightning streaks, turning the world brilliant for one second, followed immediately by a deafening roar of thunder.

The rain intensifies, cold and sluicing in great sheets across the jungle.

I turn my face to the sky, savoring the sensation of water on my hide. The rains will make it harder for us to track. A blessing from the spirits on our marriage; a sign that perhaps I can change my mate's mind.

When I turn my attention back to my mate, her knees are drawn up to her chest. Small shakes spread through her body, her tiny teeth clicking together.

"You are cold."

"N-n-n-no."

"You are lying?"

She glares at me, shuddering, as the icy rain continues to pour. "Yes."

"Come, my mate." I ignore her look of distress. "I will find us shelter and we will warm your fragile human skin."

I should not be as excited as I am at the prospect.

CHAPTER
SEVEN

NIKI

IT'S POURING RAIN. Because of fucking course it is. Just the shit cherry on top of this fucked up fudge sundae.

I'm so angry, I can't tell if I'm shaking from it or the cold. Except, my teeth are clacking together like a possessed skeleton on Halloween, and that usually doesn't happen unless hypothermia is imminent.

Perfect!

I stand slowly. The ground turns slippery under my boots, the lime-green moss that seems to cover everything proving ridiculously hard to get a foothold on.

My thoughts are a whirlwind, as dark as the midnight sky. Lightning flashes again, so near that the resulting thunder nearly deafens me. I scrub a hand down my face, but it does absolutely nothing to clear my vision. At least if I cry again, he won't be any the wiser.

I remember the last time I was this angry. The day I got news that my parents' unit had been take out during the Roth attack. I didn't believe it. I couldn't, even with the proof right in front of my face.

I let the rain slick across my skin, like it will wash the painful memory away.

The Federation betrayed us. All of us. I gave my entire life to their cause of protecting Earth, and they couldn't even give us the option to say no, tossing us into space like fertile chattel. My stomach churns, and I press a palm against my mouth.

No wonder they kept the binary comms from the Suevans classified so highly that all we got were tiny unredacted snippets.

No wonder they made us swear and sign an oath that we would do what it took to secure the tech for Earth's safety and future.

Motherfuckers.

"I can't see," I shout above the rain, and take a step forward, towards the Suevan shape in front of me, and promptly lose my footing, slipping hard onto my ass.

"Little mate," that harsh voice sounds right at my ear, and before I can wrap my head around the idea, he's hauling me off my feet, cradling me against his chest.

"My name's Niki," I say, crossing my arms, trying not to touch any part of him I don't have to. I want to tell him I can walk, but clearly, I am not made for this terrain.

Whereas the giant alien lizard man sinks his taloned feet deep into the mossy soil, rain glancing off his scaled hide as he bows over me, taking the brunt of it.

"Ni-Kee," he says, and his tone is so reverent it surprises me, cutting through my inner maelstrom of anger at the Federation.

Lightning burns across the sky, branching off into a million different directions, briefly illuminating the angles of his face. His scales are smaller there, closer together and not as harsh seeming. His diamond pupils widen as he realizes he has my attention, and a soft smile curves his mouth. I swallow hard, forcing myself to look away. Anywhere else. Even the white, flesh-eating monster flower.

"Tell me about what Federation command said. I want to

know everything." Yes. Concentrating on their betrayal, on figuring out what their calculus was—that will be a good distraction. From the cold, pelting rain... and from the heat of the male who holds me in his arms like I'm fragile as spun glass.

"We reached out to your government about a possible alliance." He picks up the pace, darting through the woods at a speed that is inhuman and graceful. My jaw twitches. This species would decimate our planet. I should be grateful they chose Earth to ally with, but I'm still steeping in my anger. My teeth are still chattering, but they slow as his warmth seeps into my soaked clothes.

Wait. Something clicks in my brain.

"Why would you want to ally with Earth?"

His pace slows as he zig zags around a tree, smoking from a recent lightning strike. Fire burns in the core of it, the moss shriveling where it makes contact.

"Don't avoid the question," I snap.

"I am not, sweet Ni-Kee," he says. "I am simply trying to form the proper words. A great tragedy that has befallen our people. It is not easy for me."

I wrinkle my nose, a pang of empathy darting through me, followed by guilt. Here I am, only thinking about my own predicament, and he's literally carrying me through an alien jungle during a torrential downpour as I interrogate him about things that might emotionally compromise him.

If I were Gen or Michelle, I could probably figure out a way to exploit that weakness. The thought just makes me tired, though.

Oh God. Gen. Gen's going to be murderous when she finds out she's been married off to a Suevan. I cover my face with my hand. I did this. I told them they had to take part in the ceremony.

And now my whole crew is married in the eyes of the Suevans.

Gen is going to kill me.

Draz sighs heavily, and I refocus on him. "Our people are declining. Our scientists have determined the cause is a virus from a planet not too far from here, brought back from a settler there. The virus interacts with our reproductive chromosomes, causing only males to be born. It started six decades ago."

I press my hand harder into my face, knowing what's coming next.

"We determined human females are compatible with our race. Your government provided your genetic material information to us, and we ran tests on them, ensuring that it would work." His voice is so gentle now that I strain to hear him over the sounds of the storm, the sounds of the water rushing across the jungle. "You are one of two species that could help repopulate our numbers. In return, we would ally with Earth, providing them, your people, with what they need to secure your planet."

I can almost understand it—why the Federation did it. But what happened to choice? Surely they could have recruited volunteers. Rain pelts against my boots, and I grit my teeth.

No, they wouldn't have had volunteers, not after the Roth invasion.

"The females are the keepers of our culture. Our language, our words, our stories... We consider them sacred, same as Sueva, our planet. Holy. Our females are our record keepers, among many other things."

"Why?" I ask, curiosity getting the better of me. We know so little of these people, and frankly, I find it all fascinating. It's one of the reasons I joined the Federation, other than the pressure from my military family. Alien civilization, other worlds in the stars... It's always been my dream to explore, to make first contact. I shift uncomfortably.

I never thought I would be married into one against my will, though.

"Because through the woman, the line continues. Our species continues. Our females are revered. Is this not the way with humans?"

I struggle with an answer to that. "Are your women allowed to fight? To hold command?" I'm still covering my face with my hands, and he gently pries them off, staring down at me with those strange, otherworldly eyes.

"Why would they not be?" He shrugs, his massive muscles bunching against my side as he does.

"Ah," I say, casting around for an answer. It doesn't seem the prudent time to bring up the fact that only hours before I was beyond proud of being the first all-woman team in space... especially considering we were only given that distinction to be sold off in marriage.

"We never even entertained the idea that they would deceive you in such a manner. That is a grievous offense."

"A grievous offense," I echo. "Well, I agree with you on that, Draz." I rub my hands across my arms, trying to warm them up. It's futile. The wet cold has seeped through my clothes, and my teeth chatter harder than ever without Draz's body heat.

He grins down at me. The rain stopped, though I can still hear it, pounding the Suevan jungle. I blink, adjusting to the dim light. Wherever we are, at least it's drier here. I shuck my wet jacket, and it plops against the ground. Draz waves a hand, and more lights begin glowing.

I squint at one, the blue orb leaving a thick, slimy trail behind it. Eyes on stalks regard me solemnly. Its great blue foot gently oozes as it tugs its house higher up the wall. Big as my head, the snails are all around us, peaceful and so other-worldly that I'm rendered momentarily speechless.

"S-s-s-snails," I whisper through chattering teeth, awed. "Bioluminescent." I'm shaking hard from the cold, and my tongue trips over the word.

The snails streak all over the cylindrical structure, and the more I turn, the more appear, glowing at my motion, the luminescence activated by it.

"We should be safe here for the night." Draz rumbles. "Ni-

Kee, you are cold. Your body cannot maintain a proper temperature. I fear you will become ill if you do not warm up."

I turn towards him, my eyes adjusted fully. The pale scar on his face reflects the blue snail lights, and I'm struck with a memory of the first time I saw a vid of him, fighting against the Roth. He was terrifying, yes, using talons and teeth and a huge energy sword to cut his way through our mutual enemy. But he was on our side, against our mutual enemy, and many humans cheered at his brutal grace.

A shiver wracks me, and his hand settles on my shoulder, holding me upright.

"F-f-fire?" I barely manage to form the word. I'm pretty sure I already know the answer, but I might as well ask.

Sure enough, he reaches out and knocks on the side of the structure. "This is a tree. We do not start fires within them."

"F-f-f-f-f-fuck me," I finally grit out. He's right. I need heat.

Shock washes across his features, and he stalks closer, his tail flicking furiously back and forth. "If that is what you wish, I suppose it *will* get you warm."

"No!" I slap a hand to my forehead. Note to self: do not use that particular phrase again. "It's an expression, not a command."

"Ah," he says, the syllable a low growl. "Are you very sure you do not wish it?"

"Yes, I am very, very—"

"I would bring you pleasure like you have never known, my sweet Ni-Kee." A tongue swipes across the sharp tip of one fang, and I suck in a breath. It's long, and from the small glimpse I caught of it, covered in a rough, scale-like pattern.

"I can scent you, my little mate. Perhaps I could help you relax as we work together to raise your body temperature."

Goosebumps pebble along my arms and neck, and I back up a step. I should not be imagining what his tongue would feel like between my legs. I should absolutely not be thinking about it.

But I am. I scrub a hand down my face. I've spent too long in space with only a crappy vibrator for company, because woo boy, am I thinking about it.

"No sex," I squeak out. "No sex," I try again, only succeeding in a raspy whisper.

"Not tonight," he agrees amiably. "Just warmth."

With that, he tugs his pants off, holding his arms out to me.

Holy shit.

Nobody on Earth knew anything about *that*, that's for damn sure. If human females knew about what the firepower Suevans carried belowdecks, they very well might line up to get here. I bite my cheeks, wondering how our resident tech expert and monster romance aficionado, Bex, is faring. I try closing my eyes, but the image of his massive cock is burned across my retinas. I crack one eye back open, just to make sure I saw it right. For science.

Yep.

It's not scaly like the hide on his shoulders and arms, not exactly, but there's a faint pattern all along the thick shaft, giving it a slightly bumpy appearance. Draz is hard, too, and my muscles clench reflexively at the thought of all that cock. *What would those bumps feel like?*

"Are you worried it will be too much for you?" he asks.

My eyes go wide.

"I thought you said you were not interested in sex? You are staring at it. It may be large, compared to you, little human wife, but I would prepare you to take it." He bites the words off with a low growl, and heat winds through me at his raw sexuality.

"That is correct, not interested in sex," I manage. "It's just. It's there. S-s-sorry." A shiver wracks me.

"Ah, my Ni-Kee, my sweet mate. You may look your fill, if it pleases you. But do it as we share our body heat, because I cannot stand to see you cold."

Right. I take a step forward, keeping my gaze clamped somewhere in the distance over his shoulder, where two snails leave a phosphorescent slime trail. Yes, this is a safe place to stare.

I take another step forward, and Draz's taloned hands grip my biceps gently. His cock nudges against my hip. I close my eyes. He kneels down, taking me with him.

"Ni-Kee, it would be better if you also removed your clothing."

I almost start to swear again, but think better of it at the last minute. He's right.

"F-f-f-ine." I pull my sodden tank over my shoulders, and it slaps wetly against the ground. My sports bra is staying. I move my hips, starting to tug down my pants, and Draz lets out a ragged groan that brings me up short.

"Do not stop, beautiful female," he manages.

"Get it under control," I tell him, tugging my pants off the rest of the way.

"I am trying," he says, his body tense. "It is very hard, considering the succulent fragrance of your cunt, now perfuming the air. Your skin is very soft."

"My *what*?!"

"Is that not the right word?" His breath gusts against my neck, hot, so hot compared to how cold my flesh is.

"It's not polite to talk about it," I say. His heat seeps into me, and it is absolutely delicious after taking off my soaked clothes.

"It is not polite to talk about how I want to taste the sweet nectar between your legs as I bring you to the peak of your pleasure?"

"Yep." I nod emphatically. "That would be *very* impolite." A jolt of desire shocks through me at the thought, and I squeeze my eyes shut—like that's going to stop it. Like that's going to stop the feeling of his hard, muscled body caging mine in. Like it's going to blot out the feeling of his massive cock, nudging at the thin fabric of the underwear on my hip.

"But I can smell your desire," he says, groaning again.

It's embarrassing. "Please stop smelling it." File that under things I never anticipated uttering in my life.

"I cannot hold my breath," he says.

"Breathe through your mouth," I snap. I need him to talk about something else, anything else. I squirm against him, somehow turned on. I should *not* be turned on.

But my body is absolutely down with it.

I open my eyes. Snails. I should think about snails. Over his shoulder, snails climb the wall of the hollow tree we're resting in. Who sleeps in a tree? We're like a pair of fairytale princesses, complete with magic snails that are making art on the—my eyes narrow at the shape of the slime trail.

"Does that look like…" My lips clamp shut.

Draz turns to glance over his shoulder. "It does rather look like a cock. If you like, you can compare mine to it, and see how it measures up."

I groan, and he lets out a small laugh, the motion sending a shiver down my spine. Not of cold—his body is burning that off pretty well—but of desire. He laughs again, and I realize he was joking. I'm sitting on a dangerous alien's lap, his hard dick poking my hip, and he's making jokes about snails leaving glowing phallic graffiti on the inside of a tree.

It's so ridiculous that I can't help letting out a small laugh as well, and then we're both laughing hysterically, Draz's huge shoulders shaking with it.

After a minute, the manic giggles die away, and we're left with the raging storm outside and the sound of my heart pounding in my ears.

CHAPTER
EIGHT

DRAZ

HER LAUGHTER DIES. She stares up at me with her oddly beautiful human eyes, the white ring blueish in the light from the snails. The perfume of her arousal continues to sweeten the air, and I wonder at it. Suevan females only become aroused when they are ready to take a mate.

But my wife, my Ni-Kee, insists she does not want to mate, even though her body tells me it is ready.

"Why do you look at me like that?" I ask softly.

Hair plastered to her head from the rain, Ni-Kee seems even tinier now. She shifts again, and I try not to notice how soft and full the curve of her ass is, how powerful the muscle underneath, despite her relatively small stature.

"You surprise me."

"Is that a bad thing?"

"No," she says softly. "It's not a bad thing."

I want to preen. I want to flip her to her back and surprise her with what I can do with my tongue. Instead, I wait, hoping she takes the lead. Hoping she tells me more of what she is thinking.

Her shaking slowly subsides, the sound of her teeth clattering together replaced by deep breathing.

My little mate is asleep.

I hold her close, gratified she can at least trust me to hold her and watch over her. Her hair is soaked, and I run my fingers through it. It's much finer than mine, so coarse that the rain practically runs right off it. If I do not comb through it, I am sure it will snarl and tangle and be uncomfortable.

I refuse to allow my mate to be uncomfortable.

So I move slowly, so carefully, detangling the wet mess of it with my talons. The rainstorm rages on overhead, the snails' light winking out the further they travel from our bodies. I take my time, braiding it back in the Suevan way. It will stay out of her eyes like this, and when she undoes her braid, it will not be tangled. A loud peal of thunder crashes overhead, and she stirs in her sleep, muttering something about can-dee, before flopping towards me.

My breath catches in my throat.

Her cheeks are flushed, and I am relieved to see the color has fully returned to her spotted skin. The spots are endlessly intriguing, sprinkled over the high bridge of her nose and across those cheeks. They remind me of the asteroid belt that orbits Sueva, visible on the rare clear nights.

The asteroids are the first thing that Suevans use to navigate when learning to steer the space-to-land craft. I spent many nights as a boy and a young man memorizing the locations of certain asteroids so that I could become the best. So that I could find my way home.

I stare at the little brown dots dusting her beautiful face, and my heart squeezes.

I would memorize these, too. Because this woman, this human, she will be my home.

And yet, what kind of foundation have I built for us?

She is as alien to me as I am to her, with her smooth skin and fine hair, and strange round eyes. The people of Earth sent her to us unwillingly, ignorant of her purpose here, and without the translator in place, she could not have known what was happening.

And without being tied to the Suevan people, she would not have been allowed to access our sacred language.

I cannot imagine sending eight valuable warriors into this situation. I cannot fathom sending any of my people into a marriage and keeping them in the dark about it.

It is reprehensible.

It is a violation.

I turn it over in my head, trying to untangle it.

We might be mated, but no matter how much I want this woman, how much I need my Ni-Kee, I must woo her. Court her, in the old ways. Show her that I will be a good mate.

No.

I will be the *best* mate.

A plan begins to take shape in my head, and I smile to myself as I watch the beauty in my arms breathe deeply in sleep. I could court her. Prove to her that I am a good mate by bringing her food and caring for her, protecting her, tending to her every need, in the traditional way.

Yes. I will win her trust in this manner. Her love. Her body.

Perhaps it will take longer than I expect to reach Edrobaz, high in the mountain jungle. Perhaps it will be slightly more dangerous than our traditional courtship rituals, what with the separatists hunting us. I bare my fangs, arms tensing slightly. This human female has captured me as surely as a hunter and a jex.

This is a desperate plan, and a small, rational part of my brain acknowledges that, for I am desperate for the delicate warrior woman in my arms.

But when we arrive to Edrobaz, Ni-Kee will be mine, body and soul.

———

I wake hours later. The snails pulse gently against the inner walls of the tree, their intermittent glow a sign of approaching dawn.

The previous days' events roll through my mind, and my eyes fly open. My mate. Danger from the separatists. The first fingers of dawn reach through the crack in the tree, caressing Ni-Kee's skin. Her eyes flicker under their lids, and she murmurs something in her sleep, throwing a bare, muscular arm over her eyes.

My tail lashes behind me.

The sun should not wake her. After her ordeal yesterday, she needs her sleep, and a low snarl builds in my chest before I cut it off, determined to let her rest. Even more determined to prove to her what a good mate I will be.

Her breath stutters, and I pause, loathe to leave her, yet set on returning with provisions. My Ni-Kee will not be able to resist the sweets I have in mind. Gladness fills me that she shared her love of them with me. More ammunition for me to tear down her walls with.

I draw my purpose to me like armor, and gently extricate my arm. Her skin is warm, but not so warm that I fear she's fevered, and lacks the concerning chill from last night.

Good.

I stand carefully, readjusting my traditional pants worn specially for our ritual. Armor would have been more prudent, in light of the attack, but we were foolish, and the thin trousers are all I have. Not my sword, nor my few pieces of armor. Just my scaled hide and talons.

It will have to be enough.

Better than my poor mate, who's lips part in her sleep. The sun's rays dance upon her small mouth, and jealousy stabs me. Never before have I been angry with the sun, but now, watching it slide across my Ni-Kee's smooth skin, I want nothing more than to replace it, to drown it out in the shadow of my body.

I grit my teeth and stomp quietly from the tree trunk.

Truly, we were foolish to not have prepared a better exit

strategy in case of an attack. Distracted by the thought of having our own females.

Females we put in danger through our oversight.

It will not happen again. My tail slaps across the ground.

The jungle swells with the sounds of creatures. Something large crashes through the underbrush, likely a troblek. The sight of a tusk a moment later confirms my suspicions, and the herbivore ambles past, unconcerned and untroubled by my presence. It's too big to bring down for my mate and I, so I leave it be, grateful for the abundance of game.

Of course, I do not have my weapons, so taking down game will be all but impossible. I stretch my arms overhead, mentally tabulating all I can bring back my mate. Meat, yes, but it would need to be roasted. And with the separatists on our trail, we should keep moving.

I am loath to bring her to my mountain city without winning her over, though, and while a small part of me protests that I am being short-sighted, I ignore it, my cock growing hard with the thought of plunging into her soft body once I am successful.

Yes. We will take the circuitous route, so that I have time to show her how treasured she will be. How treasured she already is.

I can protect her. I am not the foremost Suevan warlord for nothing, after all.

I find the solman berries after walking several minutes, careful to keep track of the hollow tree my mate still sweetly sleeps in. Dark blue-black and tinged with red, the solman berries are a rare treat in Edrobaz, as they primarily grow in the lower altitudes.

I pop one in my mouth, and the sugary flavor explodes across my taste buds.

Excellent. This will please her greatly, I think.

I tear a zitsu leaf from a nearby tree, fashioning it into a crude pouch and stuffing it full of all the ripe berries it can fit. Pleased with my handiwork, I clasp the leaf and berries to my chest, when I hear her sound of terror.

It breaks across the noisy jungle, high-pitched and ominous.

All thought of berries leaves my mind.

My mate is in danger.

CHAPTER
NINE

NIKI

I SMELL it before I see it, and it's the foul odor that shakes the last vestiges of sleep from me.

It crawls across my chest, forked tongue flicking out as it tastes the air. I gag. Its breath is horrendous. I have no idea what it is, but I lie still, barely breathing, afraid to blink, as the creature's disgusting smell overwhelms my senses.

I need a weapon. Claws sink into my stomach, not piercing, but sharp and uncomfortable all the same.

I need clothes.

I take a shallow breath, anger and self-pity combining into a potent rage. Fucking Federation. I cannot believe they set me and my crew up to be sold off as breeders for the Suevans.

And I am not about to let this nasty smelling alien beastie take a chunk out of me before I figure out how to make them pay for it while still getting the tech Earth needs.

It takes another step across my chest. A clawed paw steps on my breast, the tongue nearly touching my chin now. Eight eyes stare up at me, and the thing butts its head against me, so cat-like that my eyebrows raise.

If it weren't for its super gross breath, it would almost be cute.

Is it wondering what I taste like? About what I'm doing in its gargantuan hollow tree?

I don't fucking know, but I *do* know that I don't want to piss it off.

After what feels like an hour-long stare down, the thing creeps off my stomach, turning to curl up next to my arm. Okay. I sag, my head going limp against the ground.

Maybe it's cold and wants body heat. Sure. Cold in the jungle, which is already swelteringly hot. I sit up carefully, disentangling my arm from the creature. Now that it's not sitting in my face, it's not so bad. Short fur covers its narrow body, too small for its overlarge head, dotted with eyes. They blink at once, and the thing lets out a soft sigh, forked tongue flicking as they all close.

Something cracks outside. It must be Draz, back from whatever he was doing.

My stomach growls, and I'm about to call out to him, asking where he's been. I stop myself just in time.

The hand that reaches into the tree is not green.

It's not my alien. It's not Draz.

And when the head belonging to that hand appears, a thrill of horror shoots down my spine. A long, bony snout joins to a massive head. Iridescent blue feathers shimmer in the morning sun, and the alien creature opens its maw, emitting a strange rattle followed by an ear-piercing howl.

I scramble to stand and press myself against the back wall of the tree. The small creature with fetid breath must also sense imminent danger, because it clambers up my calf and side, finally curling up on my shoulder, where it shakes in fear.

The feathered freak of alien nature rattles and howls again, its jaws snapping. Claws rip into the opening of the tree, bark spraying all over me as it snaps and rattles.

It's going to get in. I have no weapons. I'm going to get eviscerated in my underwear and bra on an alien planet my government sold me to as a bride.

I should know better, but maybe all the drama of the last twelve hours or so has gotten to me, because I lose my head completely and scream.

Weapon. I need a weapon. How many times have I taught new trainees that anything can be a weapon in a crunch?

The beast rattles at me again, claws pulling more bark off.

This is definitely a crunch.

One of the snails next to me pulses bright blue, and I pluck the thing off in a fit of terror or inspiration or, most likely, both. It squelches loudly, the size of my hand, and I chunk it at the feathered thing. It plops off wetly.

Awesome. I've only succeeded in infuriating it. The little creature on my shoulder digs its claws into me, hanging on for dear life as the bird/lizard hybrid continues to shred the opening, trying to make it big enough to fit through.

I tug another snail off the wall, this one heavier than the last. It comes free with a squelch. Blue oozes from its gelatinous foot, and I wrinkle my nose. The furry creature chitters at me, pulling my ear and pointing from the snail to the feathered fiend trying to eat us.

"Yeah, yeah, I got it," I tell it. I'm not going to dwell on the fact I'm talking to an eight-eyed furred thing like it can understand me, but whatever.

The bird-beast opens its mouth again, and I throw the damn snail as hard as I can. Its beak crunches on the snail, catching it in midair, and blue goop explodes from it, spattering my skin.

The creature screams, even more enraged. A moment later, I figure out why.

Oh no.

Holy shit.

My skin's burning, turning red where the snail goop splattered across me.

"Oh no," I tell the thing on my shoulder. "This isn't good."

It's tongue flickers out, and it bobs its freakishly large head in agreement. But the bird creature rakes its talons in anger against the tree once more, then makes a high, keening sound that leaves my ears ringing.

Finally, its head falls forward, and it slumps to the ground.

I grab my still sodden clothes from last night, scrubbing off the blue goop from my stomach and thighs. It burns. I hiss out a breath, trying to get it all off, but the damage is done. Whatever was in the snails is like acid, and blisters are forming already on my skin.

"Ni-Kee!" a voice bellows. Draz. His worried face peers into the crack in the tree, and I throw my wet clothes at him.

"I can't believe you made me sleep in a tree full of acid snails!" Bright lights swim across my vision, and little stars dance in Draz's eyes. He's pretty—for an alien. Big and huge and muscled and his face is scaly, but ooh it is pretty. Even a human man would be lucky to have his strong jaw and full lips, his thick cheekbones and long, black hair.

I shake my head, trying to clear it.

"I had to kill that big bird thing with a snail, and it got all over me, and it hurts! It hurts, Draz. Why would you have us sleep with killer snails?"

"Because it was safe, woman," he says, glaring at me. "Safe until you used one of our sacred snails as a weapon!" He kicks the beast's body out of the crevice, pulling up short as he takes in the creature now wound around my shoulders, still chittering at me.

"How was I supposed to know it was sacred?" I'm yelling now, adrenaline still pounding through my body, along with a strange, heady sensation that's leaving me slightly dizzy, like I've drunk too much cheap wine. "That thing attacked us, and I killed it. Where were you, anyway? You abandoned me in the middle of the jungle, and I almost got eaten by Big Bird's demonic twin. You abandoned me," I repeat, startled to feel tears sliding down my cheeks.

Why am I crying?

Suddenly, a huge laugh hiccups out of me, and then another. And another. Honestly, this situation is hilarious.

"I can't believe the Federation sold me out to a sexy alien so you could make babies with me." I laugh so hard more tears come out, streaming from my eyes. "And then you tell me you're going to take care of me, and the moment I'm asleep, you leave me alone, and I almost die." I clutch at his wrist, snorting with laughter now. "I mean, come on. It's too good."

"It should not be affecting you this strongly." He shakes his head. "I do not know what it will do to your delicate human system."

"What are you talking about?" I ask, still laughing. The words slur, but whatever. Who cares? He has a translator, and he will just have to figure it out.

"I can understand you fine," he says carefully, narrowing his eyes at me. "Does your skin hurt where the liquid touched?"

He reaches out for me, tracing the pad of one finger along my skin.

I shiver. "No, no, it feels good," I tell him. "It feels so good."

Draz pulls his hand away as though he's been scorched.

"Don't stop," I tell him, near panting. The creature on my shoulders wraps its little furry and clawed hands around my neck, giving me a shake.

"I leave you alone for one minute," he says, "and you manage to contaminate yourself and bond with a zoleh. You are something else, my mate."

"Yeah I am." I jut out a hip, reaching for him. "I am a human." I double over, laughing hysterically. "And you are a big, strong alien, with a big, strong cock." I stand up, batting my eyelashes and running a finger down his ridiculously muscled torso.

His abs have abs.

A teensy part of me is screaming to stop, that something is wrong, but the rest of me does not give one single, solitary fuck.

"I want to see it again." I crook a finger at him, using my best seductive smile. It's my only seductive smile, but whatever.

"Ni-Kee," he groans, shutting his eyes. "I want to tell you yes, my mate, but this is not you."

"Then who is it, Draz? Is there someone else here who wants to look at that huge, hard dick? Hmmm?" I flutter my eyelashes again, and his gaze drops to my mouth. My entire body is pulsing with need, completely wound up. Wetness pools between my legs, and I'm not sure I've ever been so wet in my life. I need to have sex. I need to orgasm. Immediately. ASAP.

The weird little animal vaults from my shoulders, clambering to the top of the crevice in the tree.

Draz doesn't say anything though, just stares at me as I sidle closer, rubbing my cheek against his hard chest. It's rougher than my skin, but smoother and silkier than it looks, too. It feels delicious.

"Is there someone else here who wants to take that cock in their mouth? To suck it until you come in my throat?"

I never thought I'd be so glad that Bex shoved all her romance novels at me during our flight here. I am the queen of dirty talk now. I run one hand lower, where the ridges of his hips dip into his pants, and gasp as I grip the thick length of him in one hand.

"Ni-Kee," he growls, and I grin up at him, knowing I'm about to get my way. I'm so turned on that the ache of pleasure is already cresting, and I put my own fingers down my pants as I kneel, trying to rip off his pants.

CHAPTER
TEN

DRAZ

MY NI-KEE KNEELS BEFORE ME, her fingers wrapped around my cock. My balls draw up tight, already overcome with my raging lust for her.

I tip my head back, and the hollow inside of the tree stretches above me, the snails streaking across the interior. I want what she said so badly it hurts; the thought of watching her take my cock into her wet mouth is an idea that will plague me until I see it happen.

"No," I rasp, drawing her up from her knees. Her fingertips skate along my length, and I tremble at the slight touch.

Her hand works under the thin fabric covering her cunt, and fresh desire burns through me as I catch the delicious scent of it.

Growling, I jerk her fingers away from her cunt, and they come away slippery and wet.

"Please, please Draz, I need to come. Let me come."

"As much as I long to hear those words from that pretty mouth, you will hate me forever if I allow you to continue on like this."

She sways slightly, her eyes glassy with lust.

Lust caused by the bioluminescent slime that burned welts into her beautiful flesh. I've never seen a reaction like this. The snails are sacred to my species, used to increase libido by mated couples trying for offspring. I thought perhaps they would signify luck, a blessing on our mating.

I press my eyes closed, my hands still firmly around her delicate wrists.

It seems I was very wrong, and now my mate is paying the price. I am not foolish enough to think she will come back to her senses and thank me for letting her bring herself to orgasm in front of me, considering how shy she was last night.

I groan again, and she writhes closer, rubbing her hip across my cock and letting out a soft moan.

This is truly torture.

"Ni-Kee," I growl, then pick her up carefully, so as not to further damage her wounded skin. Her wet clothes follow, plopping gently on top her.

"I want you, I need to come," she says, her voice slightly panicked. "Let me touch myself."

"I cannot stop you," I tell her, and I've never felt so selfish in my life. Because I want her to come. I want to see that look of lust on her face, see her fuck her own hand until she's limp with pleasure, her scent coating my hide.

It's true though, I cannot hold her in my arms and stop her from touching herself at the same time, but I know I should not watch. I know it will make her dislike me, so I grit my teeth and avert my eyes.

She moans softly, squirming against me.

The zoleh chirrups at me, then vaults onto my shoulder. Strange that this shy creature has decided to attach itself to a human, when they despise most Suevans.

The snails may not have been a blessing, considering the lust-gripped state my mate is in, but perhaps the zoleh is a sign things will get better.

Or perhaps I am a lovestruck fool.

We emerge from the tree, the zoleh sinking its talons into my shoulder, and I wince at its fetid breath, rank from eating carrion. The scent at least serves to dim my own lust, and I step over the plumed body of the quantern, disgusted that I left my mate helpless and forced this position on her.

She lets out a low moan, and my gaze darts to her, fearful she is in pain. Her body is covered by the pile of wet clothes, but a sheen of sweat coats her skin now.

"So close, Draz," she whispers, and her eyelashes flutter.

Moons of Sueva help me, but this woman will be my undoing.

Snarling, I rip my attention away from her, grabbing my leaf pouch of gathered berries from where I dropped it. A damp heat spreads across my arm and abdomen, and Niki pants my name.

I've never heard anything sweeter, and yet, it is not really for me. I bite down on my lip, my fang piercing the flesh.

"Do you feel better, my mate?" I ask her, the words rough.

"No," she pants, her mouth open.

"I will take you somewhere that will help." Water. I need to get her in fresh water, wash the snail slime from her, make her drink it until this fever fades, until she returns to her prickly self.

I pick up my stride, racing through the jungle to the closest source of water I can remember.

"Yes," she says, squirming again. "Yes, Draz, take me somewhere and put it inside me. I need to feel you." Her hand works furiously between her legs, and then her back arches.

I slow, my gaze dropping to her in wonder.

"Did you come more than once?"

"Yes, and I'm going to, to, to—" Her sentence ends with a low moan that makes my cock throb, hot seed beginning to spill forth. Her body goes limp in my arms.

What she has done is unheard of.

No Suevan female can come more than once. But this human in my arms? She has orgasmed three times now—in a row. One after the other.

I push myself faster, both worried for her and inflamed by what her body is capable of. Suevan females can only become aroused when they are ready to be with child… but my mate? She's limp in my arms from the force of her pleasure, the scent of it driving me wild.

I want her more than ever, and right now, she would have me, would welcome me into her body as I drive us both into a frenzy.

But I cannot, and I will not, take advantage of her state. I banish the thought, and a branch scrapes along my hide.

"Draz," Ni-Kee moans, and my cock jerks at my name on her lips.

"Yes, my mate?"

"Something is wrong," she says, her eyes fluttering open.

"I know," I tell her, squeezing her to me. "I will fix it, sweet one."

I push myself to my limits, racing us through the jungle, until the familiar crashing of the falls fills my ears. I don't stop, though, only slow, tossing Ni-Kee's clothing on a flat rock, stacking the berries on top, before running us into the cold water. The zoleh swings off my shoulder, sunning itself and making contented noises.

Water sprays from the waterfall, misting above even the placid surface where I wade us both in.

Ni-Kee makes a small noise in her throat, her nose scrunching up as she stares up at me, blinking slowly.

I need her to recover. My heart pounds against my chest, and it's not only from the sprint to the falls.

My shoulders are tense with worry, and I study her pretty human face.

"Is it helping? The water should dissolve the toxin. Drink some," I say, scooping up a handful.

Her lips press against my palm, and I scoop it into her mouth. She drinks, and drinks, and finally, her limpid gaze turns to one of realization, followed by swift horror.

She detaches herself from my chest, her pink tongue darting out of her mouth.

I steel myself for whatever is to come. I have faced down hundreds of enemies. I have torn spines from their bodies and roared in fury as their blood sprayed me.

And still, I am afraid of what this little human is about to say, as if she holds my whole heart in her claw-less hands.

CHAPTER
ELEVEN

NIKI

IT'S like waking up from a dream. Ice cold water sluices over me, helping to cool the blisters the stupid snails burned across my skin. It washes away most of the pain, and all of the lust, leaving me wrung out as a moldy dishrag.

And mortified.

Draz stares at me, his expression pinched, diamond-pupil eyes scanning me.

My favorite phrase is at the tip of my tongue, but no way in hell am I about to utter 'fuck me' in front of him.

Again.

I scrub a hand over my steaming face, peek at him through my fingers, and immediately plunge under the water.

Bubbles stream from my nose. I'm going to stay under as long as my lungs can take it.

Holy hell, I have never been so embarrassed in my life. The things I said to Draz... I don't think I've ever said anything out loud like that to *anyone*, even jokingly.

The big Suevan already thinks I'm his, and then I got hit with what must have been some kind of libido enhancer from the snail goop and begged him to plow me. I groan, the noise muffled under the water, my face buried in my hands.

My pussy aches, overstimulated and sore from all the personal attention I just gave it.

My lungs burn, begging for air, and still I stay under. Okay. I need to get a grip on myself. So far I've cried about my circumstance, was near hypothermia, then managed to hurt myself by using a sacred snail as a projectile weapon.

Clearly, I need Draz if I'm going to survive this damn planet.

Shame rockets through me. I definitely just yelled that I needed him sexually, too.

Despite how fucked the Federation played this treaty and my crew, I'm still an officer. I'm still the captain of my ship, in charge of the women's lives they've trusted me with. And in charge of getting the defensive tech that Earth needs. I'm not going to leave Earth high and dry. No matter how furious I am with the Federation, I couldn't live with myself if the deal with the Suevans fell through. And the Suevans didn't even do anything wrong.

I break the surface of the water, inhaling deeply, and then submerging again immediately.

Draz has been kind, caring, and competent. He even made me laugh. He could have taken advantage of me and seeing as how I was begging him for it, I'm shocked he didn't. He has as much riding on this marriage as I do. The Suevans are looking at extinction, and I just offered my body up on a silver platter.

Hell, if they wanted to just get us pregnant and use us as broodmares, they could've slipped us snail gunk at the mating ritual and taken advantage of my whole crew easily.

But they didn't.

Draz is… honorable. More honorable than the Federation even. Bitterness coats my tongue at the traitorous thought, but I know it's true.

I will do my duty.

I will make the best of a totally fucked situation. It could be much, much, worse. Draz will be an effective ally, and maybe even a good friend.

I run my fingers along my braid, then pause. Braid? When did I braid my hair? Whatever, it doesn't matter. It's time to swallow my pride, apologize, and act like the captain I am. I'm a strong, intelligent woman, and I am going to make it work.

Surfacing, I wipe the water from my eyes and suck in a huge breath.

Draz is still in front of me, his head cocked to one side, his eyes analytical and appraising. My breath catches. The scar down his face is so brutal, and it's not the only one. This Suevan has been through it, and despite his gentle touch with me, he's clearly a fighter. Despite the scars, the scales, or maybe because of them, he's breathtaking. There's a beauty to his muscled form, to his face. Now that I'm somewhat used to the difference in his features, the snail-goop high wearing off, I can fully acknowledge that Draz is compelling. Good-looking. Handsome, even.

I blow out a breath, gritting my teeth.

I need him on my side, and I need to be professional about it. No matter what he thinks I am to him, I'm on Sueva for a purpose. To make sure Earth gets the interplanetary defense system.

"Draz, I owe you an apology."

He shakes his head, the gesture apparently universal. His long black hair slides across one shoulder as he does so, and it looks so different than mine. What does it feel like, I wonder?

I shake my own head, like that will clear it, and for a moment, we're both shaking our heads. It strikes me as funny, and I bite my cheeks, holding in an inappropriate laugh.

"I do. I didn't mean to make you uncomfortable. I wasn't myself, not at all."

"Ni-Kee—" he starts, but I hold up a hand and continue.

"And I also want to say thank you. And I mean it. You saved my life last night, more than once. You got me out of a bad situation, with your separatist attack, and then you kept me from hypothermia. And today, you could have…" I swallow, a tingle of fear working down my backbone. "You could have violated my person and my trust, and you didn't."

His features are thunderous. "I would never hurt you, my mate. Your trust means the worlds to me."

My heart squeezes. Water swirls around us, the falls thundering behind us. The zoleh curls up on where Draz must have dropped my clothes, its two fluffy tails wrapped around it. Only two eyes are visible, and it watches us with preternatural awareness.

"I am grateful to you, nonetheless."

He takes a step closer, and I'd have to be blind not to notice the way his muscles ripple, the clear water lapping around his abdomen.

"I live for your gratitude," he tells me, and when he reaches out a finger, running the rough pad of it over my cheekbone, I don't flinch away. Alarms of warning blare in my head, but for a moment… for a moment, maybe I like it. Maybe I lean into it.

His touch is warm, and strangely comforting.

I could do worse than this kind and strong Suevan.

The strange thought flits through my head, and I blink up at the huge alien. The sunlight glints off the water beading down his torso. My throat bobs, and I avert my eyes, out of sorts.

I *have* done worse.

A flock of birds take flight from the thick canopy of verdant trees, shaking me from my reverie. Bright, multi-colored plumage winks like jewels in the sun. Here, in the water, the sky is wholly visible, and the asteroid belt that circles the planet makes for a dramatic horizon line.

"It's beautiful here." My hands swirl through the water.

"I have never seen such beauty before you," Draz says,

taking another step closer. His movements are careful and quiet, like a hunter afraid of scaring his prey.

I'm the prey. His diamond-shaped pupils expand, his body so close now that his leg brushes against my calf. His tail lashes in the water behind him, creating waves that sparkle with sunlight.

"I brought you can-dee," he says.

"Candy?" I echo, nonplussed.

His finger moves to my chin, tilting it up and forcing me to lock eyes with him.

"You said you liked sweets. That is why I left you this morning, my fierce warrior human, to forage for food you might like."

Another unbidden surge of affection goes through me. "You didn't have to do that."

"Of course, I did." He lavishes a smile on me, showing sharp fangs. "I am courting you. I will provide for all your needs."

I want to press him on that, sensing an opening here. Could I tell him I want proof Earth has the tech they promised? Would he ensure it was sent there if I told him that's all I wanted?

A roar bursts forth through the jungle, raising the hair on the back of my neck.

Maybe I should wait on the tech until we make it out of this jungle and back to Suevan civilization.

"I have always taken care of myself," I say instead, then scrunch my nose, hoping I haven't offended him.

He studies me, pursing his full lips.

I lick my own, and his gaze darts to my mouth. Desire twinges through me, and I still. Is it the aftereffects of their sacred lust-inducing snail?

Or am I actually attracted to this huge alien?

"I did not mean to upset you, my mate. I know you are a fierce creature, and intelligent as you are beautiful."

"Oh," I say, my eyes widening.

"Why do you look surprised?" he asks, canting his head lower. His breath rushes across my forehead. I stand stock still, trying to make sense of all the emotions rushing through me.

"It's just nice to hear, I guess." I splash some water over a dirty spot on my arm, rubbing it clean.

His chest puffs up, so close to my face that I can't avoid noticing how ripped his pecs are. "Then I will remind you of it every day."

"That's really not necessary," I choke out.

"If it makes your eyes wide like a star in the sky and curves your lips like a waxing moon, then it is necessary, my perfect Ni-Kee."

If anyone else told me that, I would laugh in their face. But Draz is so damn sincere, his expression so full of longing, that I can only believe he thinks that of me.

"I'm not perfect," I tell him, my voice slightly wobbly.

"Ah, but that is your opinion. I am of the opinion that you are perfect for me. And now it will be my honor to prove to you that I am also perfect for you."

I close my eyes and blow out a breath, pursing my lips and trying to slow my furiously beating heart. I need to focus. We're in the middle of the damned Suevan jungle, where it seems like everything wants to kill me, including other Suevans, with a dangerous alien warlord who thinks I'm his mate.

Now is not the time to think about how much I like hearing what he's saying, or how his body feels against mine, or how it feels like I can trust that he'll take care of me.

How nice it feels to have someone that *wants* to take care of me.

"Thank you," I breathe again.

"So I have your consent to court you?" he asks carefully, his eyes narrowing.

This is it. This is the moment that decides how the rest of the mission goes.

"Yes," I say, and his fangs gleam white as he smiles. "You have my permission."

"I am eager for the challenge of winning your affection," the warlord purrs, and his tone sends heat spooling through my body.

I swallow hard, and his thumb traces the motion, skating over the fragile expanse of my neck. It's more sensuous than the last time I was kissed, more intimate. I breathe out carefully.

I may be in over my head, but it's too late now.

CHAPTER
TWELVE

NIKI

I STEP from the water gingerly, the steamy jungle air gnawing at the weeping blisters scattered across my torso. I inspect them with careful fingers, hissing as I graze an extremely sore spot.

A frisson of concern rolls through me. An open wound on an alien planet seems like an invitation for infection.

"That does not look good," Draz intones. A large, glossy green leaf hangs from his hands, and my stomach rumbles as he holds out a fistful of deep purple berries. "Does it trouble you?"

"It doesn't feel great," I tell him. "I'm worried about infection."

He frowns, still holding out the berries. "Eat the sweets first, then we will worry about finding a solution for your sores. Sit," he commands, pointing at the flat black rock. The zoleh blinks up at me, chirrups a greeting, then promptly falls back asleep.

There's no point in arguing, so I simply scoot my damp clothes out of the way and plop onto the warm rock. It's hot against the wet fabric of my underwear, and I squirm a little, trying to get comfortable. As humid as this planet is, hanging out in wet clothes seems like a recipe for disaster.

I wrinkle my nose. Yeah, that's just what I need next. A yeast infection.

"Try it?" Draz says, tipping his palm towards me. His thick, muscled tail lashes back and forth, the way it does when he seems to be feeling a strong emotion.

"Okay." I open up my hand, but he ignores it, popping a berry straight into my mouth.

All righty, then. I guess he's going to feed me.

"This isn't going to be poisonous to me, right?" I hold the berry in my cheek, not quite sure enough to bite down on it.

"You think I would poison you?" His tail whumps against the ground, his fangs glinting.

"No," I exhale. "But how do you know it will be safe for me to eat it?"

"Ni-Kee," he says, and there's a hint of reproach in it. "We did extensive research on your biology before you arrived. Our species have much in common, despite the differences in our physical appearance. I would not feed you something if I thought there was even a chance of it harming you." He's vehement, his strange eyes wide and serious.

I chomp down on the berry, and a sour-sweet flavor fills my mouth, making it water. Suddenly, I'm ravenous.

"This is so good," I moan.

"Better than can-dee?"

"It's pretty damn close."

"Will you eat another?" Draz's voice is soft.

I nod, my eyes closed in ecstasy. Wow. This is the best fruit I've ever had. Something soft presses against my mouth, and my eyes fly open in surprise.

Draz's fingers rub against my lower lip, another berry pinched between his thumb and forefinger. I don't know when he moved closer, but he did so silently. His knee nudges between where my legs dangle from the rock, keeping them apart.

"Here," he says, releasing the berry into my open mouth.

It's a little weird. Way more intimate than I would've wanted, but I'm too hungry to say anything, and I bite into the next berry.

"Mmm," I say. "Thank you."

"I like when you make that noise, Ni-Kee." The knuckle of his thumb brushes against my lips again. His gaze devours me. I avert my eyes, slightly overwhelmed with both his proximity and his intensity. The leaf full of berries dangles against his hip, his hard cock bulging in his pants.

"I think I can feed myself," I tell him. I need to put a stop to this.

"It brings me pleasure to feed you," he says, a low growl in his throat. "You said you gave me permission to court you. Let me court you." His thumb brushes against my lips again, and I open my mouth, warring with the instinct to tell him no.

I did tell him I'd let him court me. As far as courting practices go, this one is fairly tame... other than the fact that heat's beginning to spiral through me.

It reminds me of begging him for his cock in my mouth, and the heat blazes into lust at the memory, then shame.

"I think I need to feed myself right now."

"Do humans not take care of their mates? Why do you resist me?" He growls the question, clearly frustrated.

"Draz, listen." Equally exasperated, I sigh. "I think you're a good guy. A good Suevan. But I just...what just happened with the snails made me embarrassed. I need a minute to recover."

"You are embarrassed because you orgasmed three times in my arm, when your delicious juices drenched my stomach and made my cock grow painfully hard?"

I squeeze my eyes shut, wincing. "Yeah. That's one way to put it."

"Is it unusual for your people to come so many times?"

This conversation is getting out of control. I take a deep breath, trying to center myself in the moment, in the cacophony of the alien jungle all around us, the thunderous crashing of the waterfall.

When I don't answer, he puts pressure on my lips, and hungry but annoyed, I take the next berry in my mouth and chew it.

"Suevan females only come once, when they are breedable."

I cough, choking on the berry. "When they are *what* now?"

"When they are able to ripen with child."

"Ripen with child." I shake my head, and Draz leans closer, his long hair tickling against the tops of my breasts.

"Do you orgasm because you are ready to be filled with seed?"

My nose wrinkles. "Can you *not* call it that?"

"Orgasm?"

"Seed!"

"What is wrong with seed?"

"It's just... I don't know, it sounds gross."

"There is nothing gross about the pleasure my seed will bring you."

"Draz, it's not the pleasure that bothers me, it's the word *seed*."

"So you admit you want me to bring you pleasure?"

"I didn't say that!"

"Humans are a strange species. You are shy about your body and about mating, are you not?"

I pinch the bridge of my nose, fighting for patience. "Yeah, I mean, I guess so." I gesture to him. "But look at you, you are covered in scales. Your body is a work of muscled art, and you can withstand anything. Mine isn't. Humans have to cover up because otherwise we'll get hurt."

"You think my body is art?" He puffs up a little, grinning down at me.

I can't help but laugh at his pleased expression. "I think that my skin isn't as resilient as yours."

His grin fades, and his big hands bracket my rib cage. I freeze, and he turns me sideways.

Inspecting the blisters.

"This is too true, my little human. But if you think these luscious curves are not the work of an artist, then I will do all in my power to disabuse you of this notion." His hands skate higher, towards the curve of my breasts, and whatever I'm about to say dies in my throat.

I start to arch into his touch even as his hands fall away.

"Here, my mate. If you are more comfortable feeding yourself, then I will find another way to take care of you." He hands me the leaf pouch of berries, stalking away, his tail lashing like crazy behind him, whipping into plants and rocks.

My thoughts tumble over each other, and I pop a handful of fruit into my mouth, trying to find a position to sit in that doesn't hurt. The zoleh makes a whining noise, and blinks up at me with a multitude of wide eyes.

"Here," I tell it, scattering some berries on the rock. It pushes its head against my hand, forked tongue darting out. "Maybe this will help your breath."

My eyes narrow, and at the thought, I bring one hand up to my mouth, huffing into it.

Slowly, I lower my hand. Why am I testing *my* breath?

It doesn't matter if my breath smells!

I'm *not* kissing the big alien.

Nope. I'm not even *thinking* about kissing Draz.

CHAPTER
THIRTEEN

DRAZ

NIKI'S WOUNDS TROUBLE ME. The blisters weep clear pus down her sides, and I can tell from the way she squirms, they are painful.

She has not complained, not once. She is brave, this human warrior of mine.

And stubborn.

My mate wants me, I can scent it on the air. Yet she holds back—why? She is already mine. I grind my teeth, pacing on the lake shore as she sits quietly on the rock, chewing the sweet berries I gathered for her.

This would be much easier if she would simply acknowledge her desire for me. I would make her want no other male after our first mating, I am sure of that. And her feelings for me, her respect and admiration, would grow in time.

Palming the hard length of my cock, I loose a slow exhalation. The cock I need to stop thinking with. I am courting her. I am doing this right, and I must be patient.

I have always been patient. That is how I was able to rise in the Suevan warrior ranks, how I was able to claim victory over many adversaries.

I chance a glance at Ni-Kee from over my shoulder. Her body is overwhelmingly erotic, so lush and different than the Suevan females. She's so responsive already, every flush of blood telegraphed through her creamy, spotted skin.

Grunting, I steal another look. Her hair is unruly, a tumbled tangle around her shoulders. That will not do. It will be uncomfortable if she does not take care of it, as fine and soft as it is.

Silt from the lakeshore sticks to my feet. Huge footprints fill with water as I tread to where my mate sits, eating quietly. There is no brush to be had, but it does not matter. I will use my talons, grateful they can be of use for something gentle instead of simply rending flesh from my enemies.

Slowly, so as not to startle either her or the zoleh still perched in her clothing, I settle behind her.

"I am going to detangle your hair," I tell her, leaving no room for argument. "It will knot and snarl if you leave it like this. The jungle will not be kind to it, and I fear it will become bothersome."

She peeks over the sensuous curve of her shoulder at me, her lips stained red with the juice of the berries.

My cock is so hard I fear I may spill over my trousers if she so much as moves her mouth.

Thankfully, she turns back around, muscles in her jaw moving as she chews.

"You would do that? For me?" she finally asks. There's longing in the question, and it gives me pause.

"My mate, I worry about your species if simply combing your hair elicits such surprise." I smooth my fingers down her scalp, and her skin reacts instantly, small bumps dotting along her arms and shoulders. Worry freezes me.

"What are these?" I ask, staring at them in horror. Has my mate contracted some illness?

I am a bad mate. I am not doing my duty of taking care

of her.

"Oh, those?" She follows my gaze, a low laugh coming from her as she smooths a hand over her forearm. "Goosebumps."

"Are you ill?"

"No, no, not at all. It's ah, an involuntary reaction. Sometimes humans get them when they're scared—"

"Are you afraid of me?" The thought of my little human fearing me makes me recoil, my stomach churning.

"No," she says quickly, "goosebumps also happen if you're cold—"

"It's warm out. Are you cold?" At least she isn't afraid of me. I relax slightly.

She snorts, her nostrils flaring as she fixes me with another look over her shoulder. "If you'd let me finish, I could tell you why I have them."

I raise my eyebrows. It is amusing to me, this feisty nature of hers. She is used to being in charge, as am I, and I think neither one of us are used to being interrupted. I dip my chin, staying quiet to hear her explanation.

"Sometimes, when something feels good, it makes my whole body tingle, and sometimes it causes goosebumps."

"Pleasure bumps?" I ask, touching the smooth skin of her shoulder with open curiosity. "Suevans have them as well. I can show you if you like, they are all along my cock."

She chokes out a laugh, and from my position close behind her, I can see the tops of her full breasts bounce with it. I long to undo the clothing she uses to bind them. Seeing her breasts... touching them... I will treasure that opportunity.

"I have pleasure bumps," I tell her. "Along my cock. They stimulate orgasm in female Suevans, along with the xof."

"Ah. Okay. Good to know." Her voice is high and small, and I frown.

I cannot understand why her species is so reticent to discuss anatomy. To me, her body is endlessly fascinating. Different, yes, but made for me. There's no doubt in my mind. I will be able to bring her to orgasm, again, and again as she showed me she was capable of only a mere hour or so ago.

"I would give you these pleasure bumps," I say. "Let me comb your hair."

"I'm not going to argue with you about playing with my hair," she says, and to my utter joy, she scoots backwards, nestling her thick ass between my legs, so near my cock that it twitches.

Control. I must control myself. She did not give me permission to do anything but comb her hair, and this I will do well.

Ni-Kee breathes a contented sigh as I gently scrape my talons against her scalp. I study her shoulder. The skin remains smooth.

A frown turns my lips down. Where are the pleasure bumps?

I try again. Gathering her hair, I hold it in one hand and run my talons gently over the nape of her neck before combing them through her soft, wet hair.

This time, she shudders slightly, and the pleasure bumps scatter across her skin. I run a talon across one in wonder, and she shivers again.

"That feels nice," she says, her voice strained.

So I do it again, taking my time, leaving no part of her scalp untouched. Her hair is combed thoroughly, detangled, and yet, I can't bring myself to stop touching it. It's finer than the fibers of the yukyuk worm, soft and drying in shiny waves.

All the tension's gone from Ni-Kee's body, too, and she slumps against me, not even caring at the hard rod of my cock against the small of her back.

I'm so involved in the simple thrill of touching her hair, in watching the pleasure bumps scatter across her skin, that I don't notice them until it's too late.

The zoleh gives the first warning, standing up on its hind paws and chittering at the jungle.

An energy dart whizzes past where Ni-Kee leans against me, splashing into the water.

The separatists have found us.

CHAPTER
FOURTEEN

NIKI

I SCRAMBLE OFF THE ROCK, flattening myself against the side closest to the lake. That was a Suevan plasma crossbolt. The high-pitched whine is unmistakable. I plug my ears, and the zoleh jumps down, seeking refuge in my lap.

Three, two, one.

The water behind us explodes, drenching my back and sending a fresh jolt of pain through my stupid blisters. I reach up for Draz's tail, trying to tug him down with me so we can form an escape plan. My hands clench on nothing.

A roar tears through the clearing, so loud I can hear it over the waterfall.

I peek out from the side of the rock.

My mouth drops open. Draz is sprinting across the shore, towards where the bolt came from.

"Shit, shit, shit," I mutter. The zoleh yelps its agreement.

I need a weapon. I'm not good at sitting out from a fight, and I can help. Maybe it's stupid, but I'm not going let Draz take on whoever is hunting us all alone.

For one, I need him. I clearly need his help to survive and get back to my crew.

And secondly… Well, he's grown on me. I like the big, scarred alien.

I'm not just going to sit back and let him handle it.

I run my hands through the sandy dirt, looking for something, anything, I could use as a weapon. A sharp rock, a sharp shell, whatever.

My hands close over something thick and long, and I yank it out of the sand. Some kind of white bone, jagged on one end. Okay, perfect. Well, not perfect, maybe, but better than nothing. I can only hope that the bones of whatever lives on this monstrous planet are sharper than Suevan hide. Yeah, right.

I'm so fucked.

The little zoleh chitters at me, its mouth thankfully less fetid after berries and fresh water.

"I have to help him," I tell it, clearly on the verge of losing my mind. "Don't get hurt, you weird little alien thing." The zoleh settles its huge head on its front paws, blinking up at me.

Another plasma bolt crashes into the lake behind me. I grin. Perfect.

Three, two, one.

I dart out from behind the rock, sprinting towards where Draz grapples with another Suevan. Draz launches a swift kick to the alien's stomach, his claws raking down the scales. The attacker grunts, and Draz uses the distraction to force the energy knife from his hand. Its honed edge burns against the ground for a split second before Draz picks it up, hammering it into the other alien's neck. Crimson blood spills from the gash in his throat.

Wow. Seeing him in action on a screen is one thing, but seeing him move like this, like fighting is a deadly dance… wow. He's incredible, somehow wickedly fast and graceful despite his massive size.

And to think those vicious hands have carried me, have

braided my hair and brought me berries.

It's over in a matter of seconds, and I'm still running for him, where a second attacker surges forward, clutching another plas knife.

Which means there are at least one or two more. I need to take out the crossbolt alien, and since I'm clearly the target here, I'll have to play bait.

Well, bait that's running toward the action with a bone shard and a lifetime's worth of hand-to-hand combat training, but whatever.

"Over here," I yell, and the second alien's eyes go wide as he takes me in. A rough laugh leaves my throat, and I put on a fresh burst of speed. Draz growls low, sounding feral, and uses my momentary distraction to take the separatist down, drawing the knife at his neck.

"There are too few of us for me to take any joy in killing you, but if you harm my mate, I will do so with a smile on my lips."

The separatist blinks slowly, still staring at me with a slack-jawed expression.

Where is the shooter?

I'm still running when the underbrush rustles to my left. Swiveling, I change direction, my lungs burning as I ram into the reason for disturbance. It's a move I've deployed countless times with great effect, usually sending an unsuspecting sparring partner tumbling off balance.

The third attacker lets out a guttural laugh, and I barely dodge from his grip.

At least, I think I have, until pain slices along my scalp as he grabs a fistful of my freshly cleaned and combed hair.

My heart pounds against my chest, and clear, cold fury descends. Nope. This is not how this ends.

"I just had that done," I snarl, swinging an elbow into the alien's hip.

Yeah, I played it stupidly, but that's what adrenaline will do to you. I should have known better. I close my eyes, blowing out a breath, focusing on the jagged bone in my hand. The pain in my scalp fuels me as the alien tugs me in front of him, a knife at my throat.

The world turns crystal clear.

"Is this the species you would mate with?" The alien holding me shakes me a little. Leaning down, he presses his flat nose against my neck and inhales.

Draz's eyes are wide, his face slack with fear.

No. I don't need him to go ineffective, I need him to use his fear. I bare my teeth, my knuckles whitening on the bone shard in my hand.

The alien tugs me closer to him still, until my back is flush with his body. The crossbow dangles from one of his hands, and I wonder at it. Why isn't he pointing it at Draz?

Why isn't he pointing it at me?

"Do they all smell like this?"

Ew. I frown, goosebumps pebbling across my skin as he presses his blunt nose into my hair, his hand tangling around it.

Draz growls, taking a step closer, hauling the Suevan with him at knifepoint. "Take your hands off her."

"I asked you a question, Warlord," the alien holding me snarls. A second later, the crossbow drops to the ground, and I lunge for it.

Not fast enough. The alien's now free hand circles my neck, and he lets out a low chuckle.

"I'll kill you," I grit out. Yeah, this is not going the way I planned.

"She is fierce. Are they all like her?"

I do *not* like where this is going. Draz lips are pulled back, his fangs fully exposed. My odds aren't great, not being held like this, where this massive alien could snap my neck at a whim. Unfortunately, judging from the hardness jabbing into the middle of my back, I don't think he's planning to kill me.

Right away, anyway.

I close my eyes, focusing on the bone shard in my hand, the

smooth way it slides against my palm, envisioning the sharp edge of it jamming right where I want it to go.

When I open my eyes, I lock my gaze with Draz and smile. His tail lashes back and forth. "Let her go, and I will let you and your idiotic companion live," he says.

Oh, he's *going* to let me go.

Ignoring the too-tight way he holds my hair, I let myself go limp, pretending to faint.

"What happened? Did she die?" Perplexed, the alien turns me around, and it takes everything in me to wait for the right moment.

I drive the bone shard up and out, putting the entire force of my body into the motion. When it meets soft flesh, likely the only soft flesh on the alien's entire body, my grin turns feral. The alien lets go of my neck and hair, his hands clutching instinctively to his balls, where the bone shard juts from. Blood drips down his thighs.

He drops to his knees, and his expression is one of both wonder and fury.

I kick him in the nuts for good measure, and he folds over. Then I kick the crossbow out of his reach, too.

"Yes, we are all this fierce, you stupid fuck," I tell him, backing up quickly to avoid his reach.

"We will tell the others," the alien Draz holds says. "We did not know their species was like this. We heard they were weak, and primitive."

"She smells good," the alien I stabbed grunts. "Are there more?"

My jaw drops, and Draz makes a vicious warning sound deep in his throat. Blood trickles between his legs and he's still thinking with his dick?

"Are there more?" The alien manages, despite the energy knife Draz holds to his neck. "If you let us go, we will spread word of these humans."

"They may not listen," Draz says.

Is he seriously considering this? Is he seriously going to just let these two motherfuckers go?

The alien kneeling on the ground jerks the bone shard free, and I back up another step, watching him warily. "I will show them the damage she's wrought. This is a worthy species."

"They're zealots," Draz argue. "They will not see reason."

"They will when I tell them of how her soft body felt against mine, of how she's already perfumed with mating aroma."

"You've got to be kidding me." I rub my hand over the newly sore spot on my head.

The alien ignores me, grunting as he stands, dark red blood dripping down his thighs. "I mean no disrespect to your human female," he tells Draz.

"Fuck this," I spit.

"Apologies, little human." He grins at me, clutching the bloodied bone in his hand. "I would not have taken this mission had I known what a prize you are."

"I'm not a prize, I'm a person, you asshole," I say. Something wet drips down my side, and I flinch when I look down. The biggest snail-inflicted blister popped, leaks a yellow, viscous fluid.

"Your mate is hurt," the bleeding alien says. "Let us go, and we will leave our weapons and packs. We have medicine she could use. The two of us will do our best to convince the others of these females' worth."

"Swear it," Draz says, his eyes narrowed. I look between them, my mouth open in disbelief.

"I swear it on the blue snails of Sueva, may they bless your mating," the alien says easily.

"Not those fucking snails again," I grit out. Now that the adrenaline is burning off, the blisters from those stupid blue lust snails really, really hurt.

Draz relaxes a little, then prods the alien in his hands.

"Can I smell her first?" he asks, with a slightly plaintive tone.

"Absolutely not," I say.

"No," Draz growls at the same time.

The Suevan sighs, staring at me with open fascination. "I swear it on the blue snails of Sueva, may they bless your mating."

"Bring my mate your supplies," Draz instructs. The bleeding Suevan disappears into the jungle, and I run for the crossbow, pain lancing up my front with every step. As soon as it's in my hands, knocked and ready to be used, I blow out a sigh of relief.

At least I have a weapon now.

"Stay close to me," Draz mutters. I oblige, moving slightly behind him.

"We would not go back on our oath."

"You turned your back on our prince and our people." The words drip with contempt.

"We did what we thought was right," the alien says. "I can smell her…" he adds, a note of wonder.

"Keep whatever you're smelling to yourself, you weirdo," I manage. What the fuck are they smelling? Lake water? Snail venom? Ugh!

"Weird-o?" Draz repeats, clearly without a translation.

The wounded alien reappears, and glee winds through me when I notice he's limping. Ha. That'll teach him. Nothing like a little bone to the ballsack.

"Here," he says, tossing three big packs on the ground. "Take it. There's dreza salve in there, too. For her wounds."

I don't know what dreza salve is, but if it's going to help, I want it. Immediately.

"Go," Draz says, pushing his Suevan hostage to the ground.

Immediately, his arm goes around me, holding him behind him. The two Suevan separatists stare at me for a moment, and I lift my chin, baring my teeth at them.

"Fierce," one says in approval.

With one last long look, they disappear into the jungle, and I sag against Draz, exhausted and in pain.

Stupid fucking blue ball snails.

CHAPTER
FIFTEEN

NIKI

THE PACKS ARE full of good stuff, and I am beyond thrilled. I shoulder one. My skin burns where it pulls from the weight of it, but whatever. My wet clothes hang off the back. Will they dry in the steamy jungle?

Doubtful, but maybe I can dry them out tonight.

If it doesn't rain again. I want to scream or binge a shit ton of sour patch kids, or, even better, do both.

Draz cuts his way through the underbrush, the long energy knife slashing before him. Two packs hang from his back, and he moves with an easy grace, his back and arms rippling as he swings. He would have taken the third pack, too, but I insisted.

I bite my lip, following in his very capable wake.

And enjoying the view.

Not just of the jungle, but of all that hard, delicious muscle bunching in front of me. Seeing him all possessive in front of the separatist aliens did it for me. It should be a turn-off, the reminder that the alien in front of me is a dangerous species, and that he in particular is completely lethal, but it isn't.

I like it.

Something is wrong with me. Maybe it's all the time I spent in space, with Bex's monster romance novels for company. Maybe it's the after effect of the fucking snails, though I'm not currently in the seventh circle of lust hell. I mentally scratch that off the list. Not the snails.

Could be the fact that he treats me like I'm a warrior princess, his desire for me clear, his intentions just as clear. Could be the fact that he combed out my hair and made an attempt to bring me his world's version of candy.

Could be the undeniable truth that I'm starting to find the big, scaled alien incredibly sexy.

Maybe it's that I'm curious about what sex with him would feel like; if there's any truth to his claims about how good he'll make me feel.

Based on the way he moves through the jungle, the way he effectively took down the threat against us, I'm pretty damn sure that he's good with his body.

I swipe my hand against my forehead, and the zoleh chitters at me from my shoulder, its forked tongue darting out against my temple. Sweat drips from every pore, stinging into the oozing wounds from the alien sex demon snails. The jungle steams—literally steams—the heat from the sun causing all of last night's rain to curl through the air.

It doesn't bother Draz, though. My boots chafe against my feet, and I'm grateful that at least my socks are dry. A month of training in Earth jungles taught me just how important dry socks are.

Draz pauses, looking back at me from over his shoulder. "Are you all right, sweet mate?"

He's not even winded. I shouldn't be either. I'm in great shape, thanks to my ship's training room and that I made good use of it at least twice a day.

But my breath comes in short huffs, my lungs and skin burning.

"I'll survive."

The zoleh barks at Draz, and I narrow my eyes at it. "Traitor."

"Give me your pack." He stretches out a taloned hand, and I sigh, frustrated. When I slide it off my shoulder, the zoleh winding its weird paws through my hair for stability, I cringe at the movement.

"You are hurting," Draz says, his voice full of reproach.

"I'll be fine."

"You should have told me," Draz says.

"And what would you do?" I ask. "You've already slathered that paste all over them." It helped at first, and I nearly went limp with the overwhelming relief of it. But now, with the sweat dripping relentlessly from me, all the paste seems to have melted off, too.

"I would carry them, you stubborn human female," Draz growls.

"You're already carrying two packs," I argue, putting my hands on my hips. "I need you to be able to fight stuff off, too. I'm not too stubborn to admit that I'm not built for this planet, and that I need you to take point. Your species is nearly impossible to hurt, and you know where we're going."

A flicker of guilt crosses his face. My second in command, Gen, gets that exact same look when she's doing something she knows I won't approve of.

"What is it?" My voice snaps out like a whip.

"It is my fault you are injured," he says softly, the look of guilt disappearing, replaced by tenderness. He shoulders the pack. "Allow me to carry you."

"No," I say, a hair's breadth from stomping my feet. "I can walk on my own."

"Fine."

"Fine!"

He turns back to the jungle, slashing away at the ridiculously thick branches and brambles. "I will simply pick you up and carry you once your wounds have made it so you can no longer walk."

"I'm not going to faint." I snort, even though a tiny part of my worries that he's right. I don't feel… great. "I've been injured much worse than this and managed to make it back to base."

He stops completely, swinging back to me so quickly that I flinch. "When? Who hurt you?"

I go still at his tone. Gone is the gentle tone, the tender look. In its place is raw fury, the Suevan's diamond pupils enlarging until his eyes are nearly swallowed by black.

It's magnetic, his rage, a palpable thing, and it makes me slightly dizzy. Or maybe that's the sex demon snail slime.

He slams a hand against a tree trunk, and leaves flutter down. I blink.

"Tell me."

"It was an attack by the Roth aliens on Earth," I say, my eyebrows raised. "They took out huge portions of our most highly populated cities. Thousands and thousands of people died. My parents, too. My team pushed them back." I pull down the high waist of my underwear. The star shaped scar gleams white against my already pale flesh. "I took a plas pulse to the hip. I half-limped, half-dragged myself to safety."

He blinks, eyes fixed on that scar. I let the band of my under-wear snap back up, right below my belly button.

"What happened to the Roth who shot you?" he growls.

A slow smile spreads across my lips. "I gutted him. Their skin isn't scaled like yours."

A rush of dizziness holds me, the memory of his body on top of mine, the pain of the plas pulse tearing through my hip, his wet blood drenching me as I yanked my knife through his stomach and laughed — *laughed* — as he died in my arms.

"Good," Draz tells me, and he dips his chin. A gesture of respect, I realize.

As silly as it is, pride blooms in me.

"Now, let me carry you, stubborn female."

The pride dies, replaced by annoyance. "I will walk."

He grunts, clearly annoyed, but doesn't press the issue.

I don't have the energy to tell him that I'm afraid if he picks me up, I might lose my mind completely and try to find out what kissing him is like.

CHAPTER
SIXTEEN

DRAZ

NI-KEE'S BREATHING IS LABORED, and yet the female is as hard headed as a troblek, unwilling to allow me to help her. I do not wish to push her away, to lose the trust I see blossoming in her gaze, but it tears at me, the need to care for her, to scoop her up.

I will have to stop for the day sooner than I thought and tend to her wounds.

It is no matter, though. We have the dreza salve and more supplies than we started with, and I will tend to her then.

I squint into the bright sunshine, trying to get a read on the asteroid belt above.

"There are caves not far from here," I tell her. "We will make camp for the night."

"How much daylight is left? We can keep pushing."

"Woman," I say, frustration finally boiling over. "I just found you. I will not allow you to work yourself into sickness because you are too stubborn to see you need help."

"I'm not sick!"

"Oh, is that so? Is that why your pretty moonbeam skin is

now green? While this is considered normal for my people, I didn't think yours came in this particular shade."

She grumbles something under her breath, and I can't quite make out what it is, but it does not sound complimentary.

"You are a leader, my Ni-Kee, yes?"

Her lovely face creases into a scowl, and I huff a laugh.

"Yes," she finally says, gripping the crossbow tight in her hand.

"Would you have a member of your team suffer to make a longer trek, or would you stop and render aid, even if it meant delaying your arrival at your destination?"

"I'm not a member of your team," she says grumpily.

"No, sweet Ni-Kee, you are not. You are my partner, my mate. You are more important to me than anyone on the face of this entire planet."

Her frown grows even as her eyes soften. "Fine."

"Now drink this," I tell her, handing her the flask of clear water the separatists left.

"You're very bossy right now."

"I wouldn't have to be if you took care of yourself."

Glaring, she unscrews the cap, then tips it back, drinking. She starts to hand it to me.

"Drink the rest," I order her.

"What about you?" She asks. "Don't you want some?"

"You need it more than I do." It's true, and her color is already improving. "Are you worried for me, sweet mate?" I take a step closer to her.

Ni-Kee's eyes go wide as she chugs from the flask, avoiding the question. "Here." She screws the lid back tight, handing me the flask. "It's empty."

"Good," I say, and turn around before she can see my growing grin. She is worried about me, and I keep my exultation silent and internal.

I do not want to irritate her further, after all.

We continue to traipse through the jungle, the heat of the day rising the farther we trudge. Ni-Kee slows behind me. Hunger gnaws at my stomach, and I worry my mate is hungry, too. Berries do not a meal make. We need meat.

"How much further is it?"

"Not far," I tell her. When I turn back to her, her hand is raised to her forehead, and she surveys the dark, fast-moving clouds overhead.

"Is it going to rain again?"

"It may. Heavy rain is common this time of year." The sky swirls, clouds moving quickly overhead, barely visible through the thick tree growth. A noise sounds ahead, and my mate crouches instinctively, drawing her newly acquired crossbow with precise, practiced movements.

Pride surges in me.

"This is good," I tell her quietly. "It might be something we can eat. I will bring it down for us."

I squint at her. Perhaps it is the clouds and branches obscuring the sun, but her skin has taken on a pallid, grey color.

"Yeah. I think I need food," she says.

I frown. "Drink more water." I hand her our last full flask, and she takes it without argument. The zoleh's asleep on her shoulder, and I remove the packs from my shoulders.

"Sit here and wait for me."

She does as I ask, sitting down heavily on one of the packs.

"I will bring down the beast, and we will make camp. Rest here."

"All right," she says agreeably.

I cock my head, surprised by her sudden mood change. Then the sound of a troblek trumpeting echoes through the trees, not far at all. It's a big beast, and this morning I passed one up, but if we smoke the meat, preserving it with the spice packs in the separatists packs, we can stretch it out for meals for the rest of our trip. There's a coil of synthetic rope in the bottom of one bag, and I bring it along.

The idea appeals to me, and I set off on the troblek's trail, following the sound of it crashing through the bush.

It takes me no time at all to find the great placid beast. Its hide is thick, yes, but the energy blade makes quick work of the docile creature, and I end its life as quickly and mercifully as I can, thanking Sueva herself for it.

Taking it back proves to be a new problem, one I solve by lashing a few branches together with the rope, making a sturdy sled. Slowly, I heave the troblek onto the sled, then tow the whole thing behind me.

This will make quite the meal for my mate. She will accept this new courtship gift, I think, and sleep well with a full belly tonight.

"Ni-Kee," I call out as I approach where I left her and our packs. "We will feast tonight."

The zoleh screams at me, scampering up and tugging the loose weave of my pants.

I drop the branches, leaving the troblek where it falls.

Ni-Kee's curled on her side next to the packs. Her blisters seep blood and pus, and her breathing is shallow.

"No," I breathe out, horrified. My fragile, stubborn mate. How could she not tell me it was this bad?

I need to get her to shelter, and I need to get her there now.

Overhead, thunder peals, and I groan in frustration and fear as the first fat drops of rain patter across my scales. I rummage through the packs as fast as my shaking hands will let me, until I find another length of rope. Moving as quickly as I can, I throw the packs over my shoulder, then pick my Ni-Kee up, the zoleh screaming at me furiously the whole time.

Ni-Kee doesn't seem to hear any of it, and her skin is as hot as a Roth's, burning from the inside.

I lash the sled with the troblek to my waist, adjust the three packs on my shoulder. With Ni-Kee limp in my arms and my heart in my throat, I begin the hike to the lunar caves.

CHAPTER
SEVENTEEN

DRAZ

THE RAIN SHOWS no signs of letting up. I pace the lunar cave, waiting for the troblek broth over the fire to boil.

Being ambushed by the separatists turned out to be the greatest stroke of luck in my life. The packs contain not only the dreza salve, which I've applied liberally to Ni-Kee's ruined skin, but leaf from the yaven plant, which I'm stewing with the troblek.

Despite the wounds starting to heal, Ni-Kee still burns with fever, her sleep restless.

I wring my hands, wishing there was something more I could do.

As soon as I settled Ni-Kee into the cave, making a pallet of sorts out of the thin blankets in the bags, I set to work on butchering the troblek and sorting through the supplies.

Now strips of meat smoke in a pit near the entrance, and the stew bubbles on the main fire.

There's nothing for me to do but wait.

The surface of the freshwater pool is still as glass, the cave quiet save for the crackle of fire and the labored sound of Ni-

Kee's breathing. My feet eat up the ground as I pace, finally making my way to where she rests and crouching beside her.

"I cannot stand to see you suffer, my Ni-Kee." I take her hand in mine, and it's cold and damp. Her face is pinched, even in sleep, the greyish cast to her skin not yet banished. "I have faith the yaven leaves will work, but you must hold on until the broth is ready. You cannot leave me, do you understand?"

I sit next to her, wiping her brow occasionally, the yaven and troblek stew starting to fill the cave with its pungent medicinal fragrance.

"You are the most beautiful creature I've ever seen," I tell her fervently, memorizing the planes of her face. The high cheekbones and pink mouth. The black lashes, fluttering as her eyes move, no doubt dreaming fevered things. The spangle of spots across her nose. I never got to ask her what they are called in her language, and I count them now, taking solace in each spot as proof she still lives.

One-hundred and twenty-seven.

"You are brave, and bold, and stubborn, and you are everything I have ever desired in a mate. And I am furious with you for not telling me you were hurting, you little human fool."

My throat closes up, and I press her hand in between mine before placing it back on her chest.

Standing, I cross over to the pot of medicinal stew. Bubbles form across the surface, and prodding the meat causes it to fall apart into tender pieces.

Good. I heave a sigh of relief. If I can get it into her, then she will recover.

She has to.

She must.

CHAPTER
EIGHTEEN

NIKI

HOT, bitter liquid slides down my throat, and I cough on it, opening my eyes weakly.

They feel so heavy.

Where am I?

I blink, the shapes around me blurred as my brain catches up. Broth dribbles down my chin, and I try to wipe it away, but my hands won't move.

"Easy, easy, little human. Ni-Kee, you are safe."

"Where—" I blink again, and something wet and cold brushes against my forehead. It comes out a croak, but everything stretches and spills across my memory.

I'm on Sueva.

"Draz," I rasp, and he's there. His massive, taloned hand is on mine, another on a spoon filled with broth at my lips. "Feeding me again, I see."

I'm aiming for a joke, but neither of us laugh.

"What..."

"You still need rest, my beautiful mate. The toxin in the snail... it took days for it to work itself out of your system."

My head aches, my throat's on fire, and I have the most insanely strong urge to pee.

"I have to use the facilities," I tell him, too tired to be embarrassed. Fucking demon snails. His mouth scrunches up to the side in confusion. Okay. "I need to pee. Relieve myself."

"Thank the mother Sueva," he says.

"I haven't gone to the...How long?" I shake my head, but it just makes me dizzy, and I give it up quickly.

"Not once. I have never been so afraid in my entire life, and I once led a charge against the Roth on a settler planet, completely outnumbered."

My eyes are wide, my mouth parted as the big alien warlord continues, his thumb stroking gently over the top of my hand.

"Four is the number of days you have been asleep. Twenty is the number of times I have tried to wake you, spooning broth into your mouth while you sleep, hoping you got some of the medicine down. I lost count of the number of times you cried out in your sleep, and all I could do was wipe your pink face and feel helpless."

His eyes are dark, his face bleak.

"Seven is the number of times I counted the brown spots sprinkled across your nose, of which there are 127. And I have long since lost count of the number of times I begged you to realize I cannot live without you."

The low, fervent words send a shiver down my spine, and I want to touch his face, to tell him thank you, but I'm so weak. So I just stare, blinking up at him.

"What are they called?"

"What? What are what called?"

"The brown dots sprinkled across your flesh."

"Oh, my freckles." I blink. "They're from the sun."

"That makes sense, frec-kuhls, a gift from the sun." He nods. "Yes, since they are now as important to me as the many stars in the sky, and every bit as beautiful."

My throat tightens, utterly speechless.

"Come," he says, setting the bowl and spoon aside and easily lifting me into his arms.

"I don't want you to watch," I tell him.

"Humans are strange, foolish creatures," he says. "I changed your bandages for the entire Suevan week, and you are afraid of me watching you while you relieve your bladder? Bah."

"Okay," I say, and rest my head against his shoulder. "You're right."

His eyes narrow, and he dips his chin towards my face, inspecting it. "Perhaps you are not out of the woods yet, my wife."

I nearly tell him I'm not his wife, that the sham of a mating ritual we had doesn't count.

But the words die on my tongue.

If the situation I've ended up in isn't the literal human version of 'for better or for worse' then I don't know what would be.

And maybe, just maybe, I would be lucky to have someone take care of me like this for the rest of my life.

I do my business quickly, and my legs shake so badly Draz has to help hold me up.

"I'm sorry," I whisper, and he wordlessly hands me a piece of cloth to clean up with.

"I do not want your apologies. I want you to drink your broth, eat something, and go back to sleep. Do you not want to heal?" His expression is so dark that I hardly recognize my once easy-going warlord. This is not my teasing alien—this is the commander who ripped the spines from our mutual enemies in battle.

I shiver again, and his large hand steadies me, spanning the entire width of my lower back. No argument comes from me as he lifts me up, walking through the strange cave and laying me back on the sweaty blankets.

"I stink," I tell him, and furious tears well in my eyes. Good lord. No. I am not crying again.

"Your eyes are… Never mind," he says quickly, but I can tell he's worried.

"It's called crying. Humans do it when they are sad or overwhelmed or happy or angry."

"That makes no sense."

"You're not wrong." I smile up at him, and a single tear drips down my cheek. He reaches out, then pauses, his eyes wide, as if expecting me to snap at him.

Slowly, so slowly, he runs the pad of his finger down my skin, tracing the path of my tear. "What does this one mean?"

"It means I'm grateful to you. I'm pretty sure you saved my life." The words are low, a near whisper, and I half wonder if he's even heard them.

"You do not need to thank me for that." He shakes his head in disbelief. "I could not have done anything else."

"You could have," I insist. "You could have gone on without me."

He tilts his chin, his dark hair falling around his shoulders. Staring at me, he licks the tip of one fang, and a little shudder runs through me.

"Once, I considered this. Not to leave you, but to go find help. I got as far as the entrance of the cave before I realized it was a terrible plan. No. I would not leave you, not even to get help."

Right, then.

"Now, you must rest and heal, so that we can make our way to Edrobaz and meet up with the rest of your crew."

Worry surges through me, and I try to sit up, but he presses me back down.

"Do you think they're okay? My crew?" As soon as the questions leave my mouth, I feel stupid. How would he know? They're all capable, trained soldiers and officers, just like me. They have to be okay.

"I think that if they are anything like you, my fierce mate, my wife, then they are thriving."

I give a hoarse laugh at that, smiling up at him. He says it completely sincerely though, and the affection I have for him, the gratitude, grows warmer. Bigger, like a bright star.

A happy chirrup sounds, and the zoleh scampers inside the cave, bounding over to me and curling up on my lap.

"She has not left your side. I think you have a companion for life."

"Are they pets? Do Suevans often keep them?"

"No." His head shakes emphatically. "The zoleh do not care much for our species, though I do not know why. Winning one's favor is exceedingly good luck."

I run a hand over the alien animal's soft fur. "It reminds me a little of a cat. They're temperamental pets we have on Earth. Except... they only have two eyes, and one tail."

"The zoleh are likely much more efficient predators than your Earth cats."

I snort. "Probably, considering they have to live on this planet."

Small hurt flickers across his face, but it's there and gone before I have a chance to pin it down.

"You need sleep," he reprimands.

I turn on my side, wincing as pain shoots through my ribs. The zoleh readjusts, getting comfy all over again. "I don't want to sleep. Apparently, that's all I've been doing for the last four days straight."

Amused, his mouth quirks up. "Then eat some more."

"I can do that."

I reach for the bowl, but he beats me to it. Pressing the spoon against my lips, he feeds me himself, smiling as he does so.

"And tell me more about this crew of yours."

I raise an eyebrow, swallowing the bitter herbal broth. There's a piece of tender meat, too, and I chew it carefully. Exhaustion tugs at me, but my mind is awake. How close did I get to death?

My eyes shutter, and fear jolts through me.

I almost died, and this alien, my alien husband, saved me. There's no doubt in my mind.

"Ni-Kee?" he says, his hand circling my wrist, squeezing gently.

"I'm okay," I tell him. I'm nearly overcome with emotion, but I want to do as he asked. I want to tell him about the incredible women that shared this mission with me. I want to know if Earth's going to get our interplanetary defense system. I want...

I look up into his diamond-pupiled eyes, and I know what I want.

But it scares me.

It scares me.

So I shove it down, and start talking. "Gen is my second-in-command. Genevieve is her full name—"

He interrupts, trying to pronounce the word and failing miserably. A grin dances across his face. "What kind of a name is that?"

"It's French." I'm laughing at the look on his face, and then we both grow quiet, smiling at each other.

"Tell me about this Gen."

"She's our weapons specialist, and one of the best I've ever seen in hand-to-hand."

"Which one was she?" He points to his head, and I realize he's asking about her hair color. Of course.

"She's the blonde one. Muscled. Really pretty. The prettiest of all of us."

"Blonde?" He squints, pronouncing the word slowly, and I realize it must not translate, because the Suevans all have long blue-black hair.

"Golden? Yellow?" I try. "But she's the most beautiful of us all, so she's fairly easy to pick out."

"No." He purses his lip, incredulity written across his brow. "This Gen cannot be the most beautiful one, because that human is lying in front of me."

I snort, but I'm brought up short by his sincerity. It's stupid, but I'm strangely flattered, and that little warm ball of affection grows hotter.

"Yellow hair?" he repeats, his eyes growing distant. "Fair of face… yes. I remember this Gen. You say she is fierce, too?"

"Not just fierce," I tell him. "Gen can be downright mean. She doesn't put up with nonsense, not from anyone. She's a great first officer, and she's even better in a pinch." I sit up on my elbows. "And she's going to murder me when she sees me."

"I will protect you," Draz says earnestly. "But I hope she does not try."

"It's a figure of speech." I pause, licking my lips, and Draz takes that as an open invitation to shovel more soup into my mouth.

At least, I hope it's a figure of speech.

"Who did she, erm…" My mind still doesn't want to admit to it, but I soldier on. "Marry?"

"She is married to our prince, Kanuz."

I choke on the broth he's dutifully shoving in my mouth.

"Prince?"

"Yes. He insisted on having a mate, too, and he cannot be denied."

"Oh my God. Gen and your prince. Is she going to kill him?" This time, I'm not being figurative. I'm worried about an intergalactic incident. I'm worried my second-in-command will literally chop the huevos off the Suevan prince if he so much as looks at her the wrong way.

"He may be a prince, but he trained with all of us. The warlords that were chosen to wed the humans, that is. He is used to getting his way." A slight grin pulls his full lips up in a smile, softening his blunt features.

"I remember him saying that he would pick the most beautiful of the humans, but I got to you first," Draz continues, a smug smile on his lips.

I remember it then, striding down the ship's ramp, the gargantuan Suevan delegation approaching us, and the way

Draz's eyes held me, pinning me in place. The way he immediately claimed me, the way his muscled shoulders rippled, the menacing scar across his eye.

On impulse, I reach a hand up, tracing the marred flesh with two fingers.

Draz stills under my touch, then groans, pressing his cheek into my hand. His skin isn't as hard here, which is likely why he has such a gruesome scar. His eyes close, and there's such longing etched across his face that I suck in a breath.

My hand falls away. Draz's eyes open, and for a moment, we simply stare at one another.

"Sleep now," he says. "Tomorrow you can tell me of the rest of your crew, and I will tell you of my warlords. And tomorrow we will work on regaining your strength."

"And a bath," I tell him.

"I will help you bathe," he says solemnly. "I will not have you drown because you are ill, so do not think to be shy about your body. I swear I will not touch you. Not until you ask me to, my wife."

"Okay," I agree.

He blinks at me as though he expected more arguing.

Frankly, I'm too tired to argue, and I close my eyes. Draz's face swims in my mind's eye, along with his broad shoulders and muscled chest.

I may be sick and weak, but the thought of asking him to touch me is becoming more and more appealing.

CHAPTER
NINETEEN

DRAZ

I SLEEP NEAR MY NI-KEE, in case she has need of me during the night, or if her temperature burns hot again.

It's a fitful sleep, not at all satisfying, fraught with worry as I still am.

Finally, I give up, rising as the first beams of sunlight descend through the craggy, overhead opening.

Ni-Kee's sleep seems much more peaceful than it has the last three nights, and her arm flops over her eyes, her breathing deep and even.

The sunlight bathes her skin, her hair shimmering in the golden rays of early morning. My breath catches, and I close my eyes, my hands clenched into fists.

I long to touch her.

And last night, when she touched me—of her own volition— her gentle fingers running over the edge of my scar, I nearly lost control. Nearly brought my lips to her narrow wrist, nearly unraveled the tenuous thread of trust that stretches between us.

Perhaps it is her sickness, but she seems to be softening to me. Softening to the idea of being mine.

I hope it is not her sickness.

"Draz."

I turn immediately at the sound of her musical voice, her pretty lips swollen and pink from sleep. The unnatural flush is gone from her skin, and she sits up easily, blinking in the bright light.

"Yes, my heart," I answer immediately, without thinking.

Her eyes widen, and her throat does that adorable bob as she swallows. Regret washes over me. Why can I not simply control myself around this human female? But it's true. She holds my whole heart, and I pine for her, loathe to leave her side. Waiting for the opportunity to graze that addictively soft skin, waiting for her to say my name, as she does now.

"Can you help me go to the bathroom?" Her cheeks color at this, and I grunt, annoyed by her species' strange ideas of what is appropriate for their bodies.

"You need only ask," I tell her, crossing to where she sits, her eyes still wide and unsure. "Your eyes are clear today, my wife," I say, because I'm done. I'm done pretending that I can continue to be patient, or that I will deny what she is to me.

Because even if she decides she will not honor our mating ritual, she will always be my wife. And if she chooses not to, I will understand, and try to continue on without her, because she was tricked into it by her lousy human Federation.

But I will hope. And I will try. And I will not hide how I feel.

She opens her mouth, and I narrow my eyes, waiting for that familiar spark of her resistance. But she closes it, only putting her hands out for me to help her up.

When she stands on her own, shaky but still strong, I beam at her. "Well done, my mate. We will make it to Edrobaz in no time."

"Maybe not today," she says hoarsely, and I check her wounds as we walk out of the cave. They're healing well, now scabbed over, and without the angry red streaks that marked them only a few days ago.

"Not today," I agree. Early morning birds call to each other from the surrounding jungle, and a troblek trumpets somewhere in the distance. Mist creeps along the ground, clutching at our ankles as I walk her to the makeshift bathroom spot.

She clears her throat, but I raise one eyebrow. "Still shy?"

"It's just… I don't know. I like my privacy when I go to the bathroom."

"Are you sturdy enough to not need my hands on you?" If she says yes, I will not insist. I will trust that she knows best, even though my instincts are screaming at me to coddle her.

She is a warrior, even though she is human. No warrior wants to be coddled.

She squints into the distance, where a large iquid swings from the branches. "Yes."

"All right then, little one," I say easily, turning my back and letting her do her business. "I am here if you need me."

"I know," she says with a quiet confidence that makes me ache for her. Moments later, she's finished, and I help her back into the cave. The still water of the lunar cave glistens with sunshine.

"Would you like a bath today?" I ask her. Selfishly.

I want to help her bathe. I want to use the small packet of soap I found in the separatist's bags, and lather it up all over her smooth, supple skin. I want to rub my hands on her.

"Oh my God, yes," she moans.

My cock immediately grows hard. "I will help you—" I pause.

She stares up at me.

"If you need it."

Her lips narrow as she thinks on it, her fingers drumming against where she clutches my arm.

"It's hard for me to admit I might need help," she says slowly. "I don't want to be a burden."

My mouth drops in consternation. "Is that what you think of my offer? That you are a burden?"

She doesn't answer, her shoulders folding inward. Carefully, I draw her chin up, until she's looking at me, caught in my gaze.

"You will never be a burden to me, sweet wife. Helping you bathe will be an exercise in restraint for me, an exercise in worship, and likely, the greatest pleasure of my life so far." I know of a few things that will eclipse it, but now doesn't seem like the best time to bring up what she said about sucking my cock, so I clamp my lips closed and try to ignore the raging lust.

"And I can trust you to be a gentleman?" she says, her brow drawn tight together, creating furrows there.

I push my finger against the wrinkles, until they smooth out again.

"I am not gentle, nor am I a human. I am a warlord of Sueva, and I have honor. However, if you are asking I would disregard your wishes to remain apart from me, I would not."

That doesn't mean that I will not memorize the curves of her body, that I will not look upon her swollen breasts and think of them when I bring myself to orgasm later.

I may have honor, but I am selfish when it comes to her.

CHAPTER
TWENTY

NIKI

I DIP a tentative toe in the water. It's cool—at least, cooler than the warm, damp air of the cave, and I'm too gross to care that it's not bathwater warm.

The cave reminds me a little of places on earth, the one with the stalactites and stalagmites. I can never remember which are which, but the formations are the same here, long and sharp, jutting up and down like teeth. Now that I'm not burning up with fever and starting to recover, I'm curious about this place.

The cave isn't the grey or brown I might expect, but a polished white, so polished in some places that it's hard to see when the sun hits just right, turning everything inside a dazzling white.

"What is this place?"

"It's a lunar cave. Suevans come here, and to others systems all around the planet, when they wish to meditate. There used to be great temples, some full of treasure, for our people to seek respite in. They've all but crumbled now. This is a place of peace."

"Lunar cave? Like the moon?"

"Just so." He points up at the cave ceiling, where round circles let the light in. "When the moon is full, the cave shimmers with the pale light. It is a wonder to behold."

"Oh," I say, turning in a small circle, inspecting the apertures that dot the cave ceiling like Swiss cheese. Cool water creeps up my ankle, and I lift it, shaking it out. The zoleh darts to and from the edge, clearly concerned about me getting wet. I grin at its antics.

"Are you going to just put your foot in? Is that how humans clean themselves, a toe at a time?"

"No." I snort, looking over my shoulder at where Draz hovers behind me on the silty-white sand shore, ready to catch me if I decide to topple over in fatigue.

Considering how messed up I was, I can't say I blame him.

In fact… it's cute. His body is tense, his eyes watchful, as I step deeper into the water, now lapping around my shins, then my thighs.

I exhale as it reaches my breasts, cold against my nipples, then suck in a deep breath and go under.

My underwear is, frankly, disgusting, and I peel it away from my body, sighing in relief as it's finally off. I'll have to do my best to wash and dry it. Thankfully, my Federation-issued clothes are dry, if not a bit musty smelling, like everything else seems to be on this dang planet.

I surface, running one hand over my face, my underwear in the other.

"Draz?"

He's staring at me, his long, powerful tail thrashing in the water behind him.

"Draz," I repeat, trying to divert his attention from my body. I'm not scared, or even… worried, considering how thoughtful the big warlord's been.

"My wife, when you say my name, your body bared to me, it

is all I can do to not pull you towards me and bury my tongue in your cunt. You would like it very much, almost as much as you would like it when I fill you with my cock and pleasure you with my xof."

A vision of his dark head between my legs floats into my brain, his thick tongue on me, and my body clenches in sudden desire.

I bet he'd be as good at it as he says he is.

I cough gently, and his hot gaze flickers to my face.

"I will not touch you unless you request it," he says gravely, then narrows his eyes. "And you are not well enough to request it."

"Right," I manage. "Well. Now that that's cleared up, can you trade me the soap for my underwear?"

"You would trade me your undergarments?" A slow, mouth-watering grin tugs up one corner of his lips.

"Ah, it's a figure of speech. I just meant... will you hand me the soap?"

"And I get to keep your undergarments."

I duck my head under, blowing bubbles out from my mouth in a steady stream.

What if I said yes? That he got to keep my undergarments?

What if I want him to do everything he says he's going to do?

Maybe something's wrong with me, maybe it's the vestiges of fever or snail slime or whatever, but it's true.

I want Draz. I want the big alien warlord, and what's more... I like him. A lot. I can't think of one person who would take care of me like he has, save for my crew. I rise up on my tiptoes, breaking through the water again.

He closed the distance between us when I was underwater, and I stare up at him. His chiseled jawline, the complete confidence in his eyes. The scar, which is somehow unbearably sexy. The long, black hair, now drawn up into a strap on top of his head.

And he only looks more masculine and delicious like this.

"Soap?" It comes out a croak, and his smile deepens, eyes raking over my face, to my exposed shoulders, to where the tops of my breasts are visible in the water.

He takes the underwear from my hand, but he doesn't hand me the soap. He weaves the underwear around his wrist, where it looks obscene, floating next to his arm in the water.

I'm hardly breathing.

Draz circles around me, the water not deep enough here to cover the thick muscle of his chest. His tail creates a strong current as it lashes back and forth in the water. The surface is anything but still now.

"Can I touch you, Ni-Kee?"

"Yes." I exhale as his powerful hands run over my shoulders. Gentle. Undemanding. Exploring. It slowly turns to slow circles, delicate and careful.

I've just given him permission to touch me, and I expected sex. Wanted it, even.

Instead, the warlord washes me, soap lathering up on my skin and smelling of something clean and herbal I don't have a name for.

The muscles in my shoulders gradually loosen, the ache of disuse and lying quiet on a cave floor for days on end melting away under his ministrations.

He works his way over one arm, then the next, and lower... down my back, until my eyes are squeezed shut with anticipation.

One hand ghosts over the naked curve of my ass, and then his touch is gone.

"Here," he says roughly, pushing the soap into one of my hands. "I will wait to make sure that you do not fall over, but you should clean the rest."

I'm hot all over, near-trembling, and not from the residual weakness of being sick.

But from desire.

I want Draz, and I want him badly.

I take the soap, turning towards him. Locking eyes with him. The soap skims over my front, and my hands follow, chasing the thin, foamy square. My fingertips brush over the hard peaks of my nipples.

I moan, and his diamond-pupils dilate.

"Wife." It's a challenge, a command.

I hold his gaze.

My hands run lower, and I scrub the soap over my stomach, careful to avoid the barely healed blisters. Lower still, and the soap rubs over the short curly hair between my legs.

The Suevan blinks, then rolls his shoulders. "You play a dangerous game."

"I'm just washing myself," I say, and we both know it's a lie. That something's changed between us, irrevocably.

There's no going back now. Now, we'll see who will crack first. The corner of my mouth slides up, then the other one.

"I think I should wash all my clothes, don't you?"

"Yes," he grits out.

"Will it bother you too much if I'm not wearing them today? There isn't anything else for me to put on, but they really need to be cleaned." I stand still, curious about what he'll say.

What he'll do.

"No." He shakes his head emphatically, and I almost laugh. "You are the one with strange notions about your body coverings."

"Mmm," I say, the soap sliding between my legs, letting my head fall back.

I know I'm teasing him, this tightly controlled warlord who's proven himself over and over again.

"Ni-Kee," he says, and the water rushes around my legs as his big tail thrashes behind him. "What are you doing, my wife?"

"Just getting clean."

"I do not think that is what you are doing at all," he mutters, his fang flashing.

"Hmmm," I answer, non-committal. I can't stop smiling. I haven't had this much fun in ages.

Maybe I'm playing with fire, but I like this game almost as much as I like the huge warlord staring at me with naked desire in his alien eyes.

CHAPTER
TWENTY-ONE

DRAZ

THE HUMAN FEMALE IS CAPRICIOUS, perhaps meaner than I first thought. I barely restrained myself as she cleaned her whole body.

I wanted to ask if I could help her, if I could part the delicate places of her, if I could make her scream my name.

But she is healing. She is recovering, so I said nothing.

Did nothing.

And the day passed by with her scrubbing more of her clothes, parading around naked as they dried.

I could hardly make conversation with her. I shouldn't have looked, but the image of her lush, soft body is burned in my memory.

Her full breasts, tipped in deep pink nipples, more brown spots speckled across the tops. I may have counted the 127 that scatter across her cheeks and nose, but I ache to count the rest. To catalog each and then kiss them with my tongue.

I burn to taste her.

So now, she sleeps beside me, as she has off and on all day, waking to chat and check on her drying clothes, only to eat and fall back asleep.

Which is good, because my female needs her strength.

Because when she is fully healed, I am going to ease the ache in my cock with her teasing body. For now, my hand will have to do. I slide my palm over my hard length, gritting my teeth, imagining it's her soft pink one. Imagining she's licking it, like she promised she would do, high on the snail's slime. Imagining that I've spread her legs as wide as they'll go, licking and teasing between her thighs, until she's screaming my name and coming in my mouth.

And then, because she is a human, I will make her come again and again, with my mouth, with my fingers, with my cock and my xof, until she is limp with pleasure and can think of nothing but being my mate.

I work my cock into a frenzy, grunting slightly, my eyes squeezed tight.

Next to me, Ni-Kee stirs in her sleep, and the fragrant perfume of her arousal shocks my senses. My cock grows impossibly harder.

Is she aroused in her sleep? The thought sends me close to the edge, and then Ni-Kee turns over. I pause, watching her breathe, watching the rise and fall of her breasts under the thin blanket, the way her nipples peak underneath it.

When my gaze slides upward, to her face, her pretty eyes are wide open, her cheeks flushed, and her focus firmly on the hard cock in my hand.

I groan, so close to spilling, and stroke myself again, unable to stop, excited by her watching me.

"What are you doing to me, my wife?"

She sits up, her hair tousled around her shoulders, the sheet falling off her bare breasts, and part of me wonders if I am dreaming, if this is real.

When she reaches a soft, pale hand out and fits it around my cock, I know I must be.

"Let me." The words are an exhalation, an entreaty. "I want to know what it feels like. I want to…" She trails off, waiting for me, I realize. For my permission.

"Do what you will with it, it is yours. I belong to you." The scent of her arousal thickens, and my mouth waters, needing to taste her.

My body jerks as she trails tentative fingers over it, exploring the bumps of my arousal with wide-eyed wonder, the hard xof, now vibrating slightly at her touch.

She pauses over it. "What is this?"

"My xof. It sings for you, my mate." I can barely get the words out. I need more, but I am not about to rush her.

"Human men don't have this," she says. "What does it do?"

"It prepares our females for mating," I tell her, arching into her touch, unable to believe this is real, that this fierce wife of mine has my cock in her hands.

"It's buzzing," she says, and then her eyes widen. "Oh, God. I think I know where that's going to go. Oh. Oh wow."

"Is it bad," I say, straining not to spill, clenching my teeth so hard my fangs prick my lower lip. "Does it bother you?"

"No." A small, delighted laugh follows this. "Not at all."

Unbelievably, the scent of her arousal grows even thicker, and I groan again. "Ni-Kee, I long to touch you, to taste that sweet cunt."

"Okay," she says, and my eyes fly open at the word. She's saying yes?

When I look up at her, her eyes are wide and lust-addled, her cheeks and chests flushed, her obscenely full breasts dangling just within reach. My cock's still in her hand, and she squeezes it gently, experimentally. My eyes roll back in my head.

"Tell me again," I say, wanting so badly to not have misheard.

To my surprise and eternal delight, Ni-Kee's lips are on mine, gently brushing against them. Her hand continues to work my cock, and I groan with exquisite agony.

"I want you to touch me," she says. "Please."

Her lips crash against mine, harder now, insistent, and I unleash myself.

CHAPTER
TWENTY-TWO

NIKI

MY SHOCK and glee at rolling over to find Draz touching himself set off a burning need inside me, the delicious ache of lust already making me wet as I watched him.

When he kisses me back, though, utterly unrestrained and wild, it sets off a wildfire. He presses me to him, his hand spanning nearly the width of my whole back. One hand plays with the tip of my nipple, and I moan at the sensation.

He uses the opening to capture my mouth, his fangs pressing against my lips as his thick, textured tongue laps at mine playfully.

My hand squeezes him gently, and he groans. I've never felt anything like his cock. The scaly bumps all over it should be unappealing, but I think about how Draz will feel inside and excitement tingles through me.

Then there's the xof. It's got to be some kind of clit stimulator, and I've never been so curious to have sex in my life. I shiver in anticipation, my legs already shaking, and Draz breaks off the kiss, his fingers still toying with one nipple.

"What are you thinking, my Ni-Kee?"

"About what you're going to feel like inside me," I tell him honestly, and simply saying the words sends a pleasure rocketing between my legs as I clench.

I run my palm across his dick again, and he makes a hissing sound, his eyes closing.

"There is much I would do to you before you find that out," he says. Before I can answer, his mouth finds mine again, insistent. I sling a leg over his hip, my foot resting on the base of his tail.

"Tell me what you want to do," I command, kissing along the scaley ridges of his neck.

"You're going to come in my mouth," he says. "I will taste you on my tongue as you scream your pleasure. When you think you can take no more, I will make you do it again. And again. Only when you are limp and sobbing my name will I show you exactly how good my xof will make you feel."

"Yes," I groan, grinding into the thick length of him. We both moan as his cock rubs against my wet pussy.

"Enough," he snarls, and then I'm on my back, Draz's body caging mine, his eyes wild. I expect him to bury his mouth between my legs immediately, to make good on his promises, but he stays where he is, staring down at me.

"What's wrong?"

"It is what is *right*, my heart. You, flushed with arousal, beneath me, wet for me. You, telling me yes, accepting your place by my side on Sueva."

I inhale deeply, wincing a little.

His tail crashes on either side of my body, his erection pressing against the apex of my thighs.

"Say you will not leave me," he says. "Say you are mine."

"Touch me," I tell him, unable to promise him what he wants. I need sex, I need him to give me what he's promised. But… Sueva forever? Is that what really awaits me?

"You're mine," he snarls.

"Draz," I moan. He drags his fangs down the side of my

neck, and my whole body tenses in anticipation. His mouth finds one nipple, and he sucks *hard*.

Gone is the kind, patient Draz, replaced by one wild with need, feral for me.

I know I should tell him I'll stay. I know I should say yes, that I like him, but I don't. I need to check on my crew—

He nips lightly at my nipple, and all rational thought leaves my mind, replaced by sensation. His taloned fingers lightly tracing down my body, so careful not to hurt me. His hot mouth on my other breast, sucking and teasing. The scrape of his fangs on my breasts.

"I like these very much, my heart," he says, biting one gently.

My breath comes in quick pants, and I'm so turned on I'm a heartbeat away from coming already.

He takes his time though, like he has something to prove.

When he finally settles between my thighs, he gives me a long look.

"Open wider."

I make an incoherent sound and obey, letting my knees fall wide open. He leans down to my pussy, eyes closing, and inhales.

"Draz," I say, pleading.

"Did you tease me all day today, my heart?"

"Yes," I whimper, threading one hand through his hair.

"Then I think it's my turn to tease." His grin is slow and evil, and I squirm, trying to push his head down and grind up into his face simultaneously.

But he's too strong, too big, and he just laughs, his breath warm on my sensitive flesh.

"This cunt is so wet for me. I've never seen anything like this."

He raises his hand to his mouth, then neatly bites one long talon off, then another.

Oh. Oh shit.

"Look at how pink and shimmering you are," he says, a note of wonder in his voice.

"Draz, please," I say. My legs are shaking in earnest now, and I reach my own hand down, trying to relieve some of the ache.

"No," he snaps, capturing my wrist, then licking the underside with his strange, bumpy tongue. "This is mine."

"Then do it," I beg, wiggling my hips.

He clamps one hand on my hip, pinning me in place, and lowers his face.

"Yes," I tell him. "Please."

"Hmm," he says. "Not yet." He slides the blunted tip of one finger through my pussy, and I get hot all over. "So soft. So smooth."

"Draz."

"That's right," he growls, eyes fixed on me. "That's who you belong to, mate. Say it again."

I clamp my lips shut, and he snarls again, a wicked and wild sound. He adds another finger, rubbing my clit between the two of them. I arch my back, trying to get more friction, more anything, but he holds me too tightly for me to get anything but frustrated.

When he runs the pad of one finger lightly down my clit, then the other, I half-sit up, crying out.

"That's it," he tells me, diamond-pupils so large the green of the rest of his eyes is nearly blotted out. "Tell me who this belongs to. Tell me you're mine."

I fall back onto my elbows, and the bastard does it again, toying with my clit.

"Ni-Kee, you are a stubborn female," he growls. "But I can wait no longer to taste this cunt."

He dips his head, that long, strong tongue darting out, and I nearly scream. Holy shit. Nothing has ever felt this good, this intense. He thrusts one finger inside me, and growls against my pussy, repeating the motion, until I'm about to crest, about to fall apart.

Then he stops.

"Draz," I moan, strung out and needy. "Please."

"Tell me you're mine." That tongue darts out again, licking, licking, teasing. Another finger thrusts in me, and he pumps once, twice.

"Tell me."

"I'm close, so fucking close," I moan.

The tongue stops, and I grit my teeth, so close to the edge that I'm going to yell with frustration and need both.

Draz tongue darts out, circling my clit, and my hands tangle in his hair.

"Yours," I say. "I'm yours."

An animalistic noise tears from him, and then he's straddling me, the thick tip of his cock poised at my entrance.

"Yes," I sob. "Please, Draz. Yours, I'm yours."

He thrusts into me, and there's no patience to it, no waiting for me to adjust. It's brutal, and savage, and every fucking inch feels like heaven.

When his xof begins vibrating, growing harder against my clit, I lose any remaining semblance of control.

"Draz, Draz, Draz," I half-chant, half-cry, feeling like the pleasure is going to tear me apart. He's so thick, the texture of him so intense, the vibration.

"That is right, my wife. That is right, my mate," he says, his tone savage. "Come apart on my cock."

And I do. My fingers scrabble against the huge muscles of his arms, reveling in the power of his body, arching against him, wet and wanton.

"So perfect," he grunts, lowering himself onto me, cradling my head as I fall back, limp.

But he doesn't stop, the vibrating xof doesn't stop, and soon, I'm riding a second wave to the top. I fling my legs around his waist, meeting every hard thrust.

"Say it again," he demands.

"Yours, Draz, all yours." Reality seems to shatter against the words, against the power of my second orgasm, and all I see are stars.

"My seed will fill you now, my mate, and you will bear us many babes."

My eyes fly open, pleasure giving way to panic. "Wait, wait, I don't know if I'm ready for—"

His gaze is fixed on me, and the savage look is replaced by one of utter sadness. He withdraws from my body, and then his body and face go taut as he comes all over my stomach.

"I'm sorry," I say, my voice small. That was the whole reason he wanted me, and it's clear from the disapproving look on his face.

"Do not worry yourself, my heart. Let me clean you up."

I should feel amazing. That was by far and away the best sex of my entire life. My body is completely limp.

But as Draz starts to wipe away the messy evidence of it, a pang of guilt goes through me.

As well as suspicion.

What if all his sweet words, all of his kindness, is all a ploy? All to get me pregnant?

I don't want to stop having sex with him… now that we've done it once, I have a feeling that I'm going to get addicted to it, and quickly.

But I need to be smart about this—strategic. He wants babies.

I don't know if I want babies, not just with him, but with anyone.

And I need to make sure Earth gets the tech they promised.

"My mate, you are beyond words. Beyond anything I've ever thought I could have in this life or the next," Draz tells me, curling me into his big, muscled body. "I am so grateful you have decided to be mine."

I close my eyes. "Yeah," I choke out, nearly beyond words.

Because I did. I told him I was his.

What have I done?

CHAPTER
TWENTY-THREE

DRAZ

ROCK CRUNCHES under my feet as I leave the cave, where my Ni-Kee sleeps peacefully. A troblek rumbles in the distance, and a flock of scarlet and indigo birds take wing, disturbed by the noise. All around me, the jungle stirs to life, full of promise for a new day.

My tail lashes behind me.

I should be pleased, thrilled, even, with finally convincing Ni-Kee to accept me as her mate. Even now, the memory of her body clenching around my cock makes me hard, my lust for her hardly slaked.

No. If anything, my desire for her has grown exponentially.

I gnash my teeth, continuing off, in search of more of the sweet berries Ni-Kee seemed to like so much.

What have I done wrong?

I brought her great pleasure, that much is certain. I never knew a female could taste so sweet, could feel so good beneath me. I thought she wanted to be with me, that she wanted to bear my young.

Instead, her eyes went wide, her face pale with terror, and she told me no.

Does she not want me? Have I done something to make her think I will not be a good mate or father to our children?

My heart aches, and I rub a fist against my chest, pausing from the pain of it, before setting off again. I know I am not human, not even close to it, but after the way they treated her, throwing her at me and my men without so much as asking her what she wanted...

Aren't I better than her human options?

A small hand tugs at my pant leg, and when I look down, the zoleh chitters at me, its bright eyes blinking one after the other.

"Did I do something wrong?" I ask it. The little zoleh just stares though, no answer forthcoming. The humans were deceitful to their own warriors. They lied to my mate and her crew about their mission. It is so at odds with our Suevan ways. We can lie, but it is considered a grave crime. Our language is sacred, and built for telling truths, for speaking from our souls.

The humans seem to feel no such compunction towards honesty.

It seems a human trait, to lie and deceive where it suits them.

The thought brings me up short, and the ache in my chest grows uncomfortably tight.

Could it be that my Ni-Kee only had sex to appease me? To ensure that I take her safely to her crew at Edrobaz, and to try to make sure that her species gets the tech they so fervently desire?

It hurts. The mere possibility that she only had sex with me because I wanted it, and not because she wanted to be mine... My throat constricts, and I suck in a breath.

I nearly stumble across the berry bush, so preoccupied with the thought, and I manage to squash half. The rest go into the bag I brought along.

Is it possible that she could have falsified her desire? I scented it on her, but every day, I realize I know less and less about the humans and their culture. Shame washes over me, and I trudge back to the lunar cave where my mate sleeps, the cave where I spent the four days without sleep, in constant vigil over her fevered body.

The worst, deepest part of my shame is that I would not take it back.

I will treasure the memory of my night with Ni-Kee for the rest of my existence, no matter the taint of sadness now attached to it.

And I will not give up hope that I can court her, that I can convince her to accept me, and Sueva.

I just have to try harder.

My back stiffens, and I roll my shoulders. A Crigomar lets out a terrifying bugle, and I crouch instinctively, trying to gauge how far it is. A second bugle crashes across the jungle, and the zoleh claws up my leg, nestling against my neck, its little hands clutching fistfuls of hair.

Two of them, then. A hunting pair.

"They sound far enough away," I tell it, and it makes a high whimper in my ear. "Do not fear, little zoleh. We will not cross paths with the Crigomar today."

Or tomorrow, or at all, if our luck holds.

The furry body continues to quiver, however, and I make soothing noises at it as I continue the short walk back to camp.

It is strange the Crigomar are active in this area. They usually keep to lower swamps, off this range and away from our inhabited areas. I purse my lips. It is not good that they are so close. We cannot afford to lose more Suevans, and the Crigomar are efficient and brutal hunters, especially in pairs.

My fangs worry my lower lip.

I may not have the time needed to continue courting my mate. If the Crigomar encroach on our cities, I need to warn my people, so that they can prepare to evacuate or fight.

I heave a sigh. Between the separatists and the Crigomar it is a less than ideal situation.

The cool, damp air of the cave greets me, and I step further inside. To my surprise, Ni-Kee sits at the fire, stoking it and eating a piece of smoked troblek. Her face is troubled, and she does not look up when I enter, as though she is so absorbed in her thoughts that she does not hear me.

The zoleh vaults from my shoulder, clearing the distance to my mate in record time.

"Hi there," she says softly, and the creature climbs into her lap, rubbing its furry head against her and sighing in contentment. "Where have you been? I was worried about you," she tells it, and a pang of sadness knifes through me.

She would be good with our children. Why does she refuse me?

I want to ask her, I want to know what is going through her beautiful, brave head, but I am afraid.

For once in my life, I am cowardly.

Because I do not want to hear that she finds me unsuitable, or that she is disgusted by my scales or the idea of mating a Suevan. I do not want to hear that she wants to leave me here and head back to the people who sold her like livestock to us.

So I sit next to her, dig through the bag, and offer her the choicest berries in silence.

"Good morning," she says, her eyes finally cutting to me.

"Is it?" I ask, furrowing my brow. "Are you well, then?"

"Oh." She takes a bite of her meat and chews slowly. The zoleh's eyes grow wide, and Ni-Kee smiles at it before giving it a piece of meat, too. "It's a saying. It's a greeting on Earth, I mean. It doesn't necessarily mean that you are good."

I frown. "So you are not well? Is your fever returned?"

"No." She grins up at me, and I start to smile back at her, loving the way she looks when she is pleased, but stop, my heart hurting all over again. "I am fine. It just doesn't necessarily mean that."

"Human language and customs are strange."

She laughs, raising one eyebrow. "You're not wrong."

"So I am right?"

"Not necessarily." One shoulder lifts as she shrugs.

"Your words do not always match your thoughts and intentions," I say without thinking.

The smile and openness on her face shutters, and she takes another bite.

I should not have said that. I scrub a hand over my face. Now she likely thinks I am attacking her choice last night, or that I am angry with her. I am doing neither, but talking to this woman is like navigating a minefield. She sees intention where there is none, or she misinterprets my words and questions.

I wonder if all the Suevans are encountering such problems with their new brides.

"I do not mean to judge," I say quietly, helping myself to some of the berries. "It is only different from Suevan language. It is why we consider our language sacred and communicate in binary with other species."

"Suevans can't lie?"

"No, we can. But it is considered a gross misstep and dishonorable."

"So you think humans are without honor?" Her eyebrows are raised, her tone prickly. The zoleh looks between us, as though sensing the shift in our mood, and runs off into the darker recesses of the cave.

"No, my sweet Ni-Kee, that is not what I meant." I shake my head, frustration growing. First she does not want to accept my seed, does not want to accept me fully as hers, after telling me she is mine, and now she seeks to misread my words again.

I stand abruptly, unable to continue the conversation. "I brought you more can-dee berries, because I know you enjoy them. My Ni-Kee, I want you to be happy. I long for your smiles the way I long for water on a day without rain. I do not think you are happy now, and I think it is because of me. I am going to find some fresh meat and food to bring back. I hope you rest while I am gone. I am leaving you the crossbow in case you have need to defend yourself, but you should be safe here. I will return shortly."

I chance a glance at her. Her expression is as thunderous as the sky after lightning, but she does not respond. Swiftly, I take a different pack, throwing it over one shoulder.

My legs take me back out of the cave before she thinks of something to say that will hurt us both.

CHAPTER
TWENTY-FOUR

NIKI

I'M MAD. It's stupid, and probably childish, but I'm so damn angry right now, and not even at Draz.

How could I be mad at him?

He hasn't done anything wrong. I mean, yes, he did marry me without my consent, but he didn't know I didn't understand. And last night, he listened when I asked him not to... I swallow hard, pressing the palms of my hands against my eyes. When I asked him not to impregnate me, he stopped.

He's been an incredible partner so far. I literally could not ask for anyone better to have been paired up with in this violent, alien jungle, than Draz. He's a brutal and efficient killer, and yet, he's charming and kind with me, his gentleness so at odds with the vids we'd seen of him butchering his way across the battlefield.

And the sex was out of this world. *Literally*.

I snort, then pop a handful of berries into my mouth. They're not sour gummies, but they are pretty fucking delicious. The fact that Draz went out of his way to get them for me, that he knows

I love candy and wants me to have what I love… It makes them taste all the sweeter.

I hate that he's right, too.

I hate that humans are deceptive, that everything about this situation was manufactured because the Earth Federation lied to the Suevans and lied to me and my crew to get what they want.

I don't hate him, though.

I hate the Federation for what they've done to me. They tossed me and my career away like trash, like my only worth is in my ability to reproduce. It's so fucking archaic, and yet humans seem to think we're the only worthwhile species.

I stand up, unable to sit with my feelings any longer, and begin to pace.

The Federation doesn't want me; they don't expect me to come back. In fact, if I did, they'd probably consider that to be treason, considering they need us to smooth diplomatic relations. Not to mention, if word got out on Earth that they essentially sold me and my crew to the Suevans, the Federation would likely start gunning for us in retaliation. Our word against theirs, and we can say goodbye to any chance of a happy ending on Earth.

I pace, ending up at the shore of the deep, placid pool that spans the center of the cave. My reflection stares back at me, her face lined with worry.

Returning to Earth is out of the question.

There are other planets, other settlements.

I look over my shoulder, to the cave entrance where Draz disappeared out of only minutes ago, swallowed by the riot of green jungle. I like Draz.

Part of me wants to believe that he likes me, too, and not just for the fact that I can reproduce with his species. A frisson of heat goes through me at the memory of last night, at the incredible way our bodies fit together, of how he was more concerned with my pleasure than his, at the way he *wanted* me.

I wanted him, too.

I swallow hard, toeing a line in the sandy bank. Ripples spiral out from where my toe nudges the water, distorting my image on the once-glassy surface.

I've never met anyone like Draz, much less had feelings for anyone like him. Intense, shockingly strong feelings.

I need to talk with him. I nod at my reflection, and she nods back. I don't have a lot of options, but Sueva is one of them. Staying with Draz is one of them.

Maybe there's still hope for me here, on this planet, if I can figure out how to tell him I'm not ready to have kids. If he still wants me in spite of that, then maybe... maybe we have a chance.

I cross my arms over my chest, hugging myself.

I want to give us a chance.

――――

I'm going out of my mind with boredom by the time Draz returns. I've sorted the remaining supplies in our stolen packs, washed and hung to dry the thin blankets, which they sorely needed, and even managed a quick nap after eating a few hand-fuls of berries.

But mostly, I've been trapped in the cave with my thoughts, and they weigh on me. The zoleh didn't prove a great conversa-tional partner, but it didn't seem too offended by me practicing what I was going to say to Draz for the last hour or two.

"Hi," I tell him, my surge of happiness at seeing him warring with my trepidation at telling him what I'm thinking. It comes out strange and high-pitched as a result, and I clear my throat, trying again.

"Hi," I repeat, then scowl. Great. I'm definitely playing it cool.

Draz shoots me a concerned look. "Are you fevered again?"

"No," I say quickly. The zoleh runs back and forth between us, chattering happily at Draz. "She's glad you're back."

"Is she the only one glad I have returned?" he asks, caution shadowing his question.

"No."

The grin he gives me is slow, relieved, and real.

I bite my cheeks, and the next words spill forth from my mouth in a rush. "I want to talk to you. I think we need to talk about... last night. And—" I wave my hand in front of me in a nonsensical gesture. "—and the future. For us. Please."

"You sound very serious, Ni-Kee."

Not my Niki, not my heart, not my mate. Just Ni-Kee. A crack forms along my chest, and I press my palm to my collarbone, wrapping my other arm around my waist.

"It is serious."

"I need to clean the fish I brought for dinner," he says, holding several up.

"Whoa." Momentarily taken aback, I stare at the two-foot long fish dangling from his hand. "That's a lot of fish."

"You need your strength, and so do I."

"Thank you," I tell him.

"It is my duty and honor to provide for you. No thanks are necessary." The words are stiff, and full of hurt. Based on what he told me earlier, they're true, too. He wants to take care of me. I've always prided myself on my independence, but the truth of Sueva is that I do need his help.

Even if it rankles sometimes. I scrunch up my nose, inhaling deeply.

"Can I talk while you clean the fish? I just... I need to get it out."

"And you will speak true with me, Ni-Kee?"

I blow out a breath. "Yes. I know you don't think highly of humans, and frankly, we deserve that."

He clucks his tongue, making a strange, low noise in his throat of disapproval as he kneels on the cave floor. The fish slap wetly against a rock, and he primes the long energy knife before slicing into one.

"But I have never tried to lie to you." I purse my lips, recalling our time together. I spread my hands, starting to pace again. The zoleh sits opposite Draz, clearly begging for fish, its demeanor so reminiscent of a cat I had growing up that my heart twists a little in nostalgia.

If I stay here, I'll never see a cat again.

It's a stupid thought, considering I've never had the time or space to take care of one.

I inhale deeply, trying to collect my scattered thoughts.

"Draz, I care for you." My nose scrunches. "Deeply."

"You hold my whole heart in your hands," Draz says simply, and his eyes are full of a wounded longing that cuts right through my core. "I have always longed for a mate, but I never knew that I would have one as perfect as you."

"Draz," I say, sinking to my knees next to him. My hand twitches in my lap. I want to touch him, but I don't. "You have to understand. All of this is new to me, and while that's not a bad thing, I need time. I never expected to be married, hell, I never thought I wanted to get married."

He keeps working at the fish, his face stony. The only indication he's listening is his tail, twitching behind him furiously.

I swallow hard and continue. "I'm still coming to grips with the fact that the people I entrusted my career and life to sold me out."

"I would not have you if you are not willing, Ni-Kee."

An irritated groan slips out of me. "Can you just let me finish?"

His gaze slides to me, a hint of amusement in his eyes. "So fierce."

"I was willing last night, Draz. What we did…" I pause, heat rolling through me in a heady wave of desire. "Last night was incredible. Truly. I loved it. I love what we have." My voice is earnest, the words rushing out of me before I can think them through, my carefully practiced speech tossed out the window, my emotions to strong now. "I think I could love you Draz, really. But it's only been a few days. And I'm not ready for babies." A little sob chokes out of me.

Draz stops, his hands still, his entire focus on me.

I push on, trying to get everything out. "I know that's what you need us for, me and my crew. For babies and for your species. And I mean, I get it. I get that. But I am not ready to be a mom. If you only want me because you want children, then I'm not the woman for you. I don't know if I'll ever be ready. I had my whole life ahead of me. I had a career. Now I'm just supposed to pop out babies?" I shake my head. "I need time. I want you. But not if you only want me for that."

He stands up, not even looking at me, and grabs the fish, skewering it with an expert motion and placing it over the fire. Without another word, he heads for the pool, splashing into it.

I rock back on my heels, hanging my head. So that is all I am to him. A vessel for more children. I place my hand against the curve of my stomach, wondering what it would be like to be pregnant, and knowing beyond a shadow of a doubt I am not ready for it. I barely know Draz.

The sound of splashing water rushes over me. He's so irritated he must have randomly decided to go for a swim to get away from me.

I close my eyes. It hurts. I didn't expect it to hurt so much.

But I know who I am, and what I want, and I'm more than a vessel, more than my potential to make babies. Shouldn't that matter?

It does to me.

If Draz can't understand that, then this isn't going to work. No matter how much it hurts, I won't ever be happy with someone who wants that of me, who demands that of me.

Breathe in, breathe out.

I focus on my lungs filling, flooding my system with air, trying to calm myself down. I said what I needed to say. I spoke my truth, like he asked.

If he has a problem with that truth, then that's on him. It is what it is.

"My Ni-Kee," Draz says, kneeling next to me.

I turn to stare up at him, my hands folded in my lap.

His expression is full of love, of affection and warmth, but it fades to something like irritation as he looks away, and my heart fractures.

"You are right. I do want children. I want a family, and to ensure the survival of my species. That is my duty and my desire both."

My knuckles whiten in my lap. I'm not surprised, but disappointment wracks me.

"But, Ni-Kee, I meant what I said." His clean hands cup my chin and he tugs me close to him, so that I'm in his lap, pressed up against the solid wall of his chest. "You have my heart. If you are not ready for children, then of course we will wait. And if you decide you are never ready for them, I will treasure the ability to greedily take all of your time to myself. You are bold, and brave, and beautiful, and I would be a fool to throw that away."

His big hands slide to the nape of my neck, and I bite my lower lip, truly shocked now.

"Last night... I thought you were rejecting me, my heart. I did not think that it was the idea of children you reacted to, which was short-sighted of me, yes? But you want me, my mate? You accept our bond, our marriage?"

His voice is so full of hope, full of love, that I sniffle, on the verge of tears.

"No, do not make the eye water again." Distressed, he pokes at my eye with a careful finger. "Is this a sign of sadness or happiness?"

"Happiness." I laugh, and then his mouth closes over mine, cutting off the sound.

He smooths his hands down my back, tugging up my Federation issue tank. His scales rasp against my skin, and I shiver at the sensation. When his talons skate across my spine, I arch into him, and he murmurs my name against my neck, his tongue exploring the smooth column of my neck.

"I like when you are happy," he says, his hands pulling at the bottom of my sports bra. I pull it over my head, and as I stretch my arms up, his mouth locks over one nipple, sucking hard.

I gasp, rocking into him, instantly wet.

"I like that sound, my Ni-Kee." He traces a talon gently over a nipple, then the other. "And I love these. I love these very much."

"Draz," I moan, already way too turned on.

"Take off your pants," he says, his tone brooking no argument, exciting me even more. I don't want to think too hard about how I like when he's bossy with me, how I like it when he tells me what to do.

I stand up, my hands working at the fastener, then let them drop in a pool at my feet.

He groans, eyes raking over my now naked body.

"I like this hair here," he says, combing through the short hair between my legs with those dangerous and skilled talons. "Spread your legs for me, mate," he all but growls, and I comply with a shudder.

"Not so stubborn now, are you?" He grins up at me, and I raise my chin imperiously. "I can scent your delicious arousal. I want to coat my tongue in it."

My breath comes in short bursts, and yet, he doesn't move, his gaze sliding over my bared body possessively.

"What are you waiting for?" I finally ask him.

"For you to tell me what you want." His diamond-pupils expand, and I know he's just as excited by the tension between us as I am.

"I want you to stand up," I tell him. He cocks an eyebrow, then smooths a hand over his dark hair, complying.

"Take off your pants," I command, loving the way his stomach flexes as he moves. When he pulls his pants down, my attention goes straight to the hard length of him, and I shudder at the memory of how incredible it felt inside me. How incredible he felt, all over me.

"Does it please you?" he asks, and his cock jerks as I take it in my hand.

"Let me show you how much." His head falls back as I lick the head of his cock, his low moan the only encouragement I need to take him deeper. It's too big to take the whole way in my throat, but I ease into it, enjoying the way his hand spasms on my head.

I'm going to rock his world.

CHAPTER
TWENTY-FIVE

DRAZ

I CANNOT THINK. There is nothing outside her mouth around my cock, the slick slide of her tongue around my xof.

"Mmm," she hums, and my balls draw up tight, my control razor thin.

"Ni-kee," I moan.

"You like that?" When she smiles up at me, my cock still on her lips, my control snaps.

"More." The word is ragged, and for a moment, I think my stubborn mate will refuse me, will not like the depths of my need. Instead, she lets out a moan of her own, her arousal growing stronger.

I curl my hands in her hair, and the scent of her desire fills the air.

Her lips fit over the tip of my cock, and then she's working it hard, her lush, wet mouth pumping up and down, taking it so deep I can hardly breathe.

"My mate," I groan. "Wait."

She pauses, drawing back on her heels, my cock leaving her mouth with a wet pop.

"Get on your hands and knees," I snap out, my need for her so strong, so immediate, I worry it will overwhelm her.

Her reddened lips part, and to my surprise and gratification, she obeys, lifting her ass in the air, her pretty cunt wet with her lust.

I lower myself to my knees, running a finger through her folds as she moans my name.

"Are you going to come hard for me, my mate? Are you going to show me how much your body loves being mine?"

"Yes," she says, and I growl my approval, pumping my fist down my cock before lining it up with her core and thrusting in deep and hard.

I cover her body with mine, my tail winding around our legs, nudging down the soft hair to the center of her pleasure. When I find it, I run the tip of my tail over it again, using one hand to support myself and the other to tweak her peaked nipples.

"You're mine," I growl against her ear, and she rewards me by arching her back, driving me deeper inside her.

I work her with my tail, my cock hammering into her, my fingers tweaking her nipples hard enough that she cries out.

When she comes, it's with a breathy moan and a flood of delicious juices.

I want to taste them all. Snarling again, I flip her onto her back and spread her wide, lapping through her cunt as she grinds against my face, making small, needy noises.

I have no gentleness in me, not this time. Not when I need to slake my desire in her, prove that her pleasure is mine alone.

The thought snaps something in me, and I hike her feet onto my shoulders, hammering into her body. She clenches around me, her eyes wide and locked on mine as she matches my hard, demanding rhythm.

"This is how it will be," I tell her, my jaw tight, my fangs grinding against my lower teeth. "You and me, my heart. You are mine, and I will give you as much pleasure as your body can handle."

She arches off the ground, tugging my mouth to hers and sliding her tongue inside.

It drives me wild, and I pick up the pace, my xof vibrating harder and harder. Her blunt fingernails scrape down my back, and I reach the peak of that delicious pleasure.

"Ni-Kee." I yank myself out of her, then paint my hot seed across her trembling stomach.

I want to shove it inside her, push it deep in, and see her swell with our child. I don't though, squeezing my eyes shut until the possessive impulse passes, and draw her into my arms instead.

She smiles up at me, a contented, sleepy grin, that fills me with a soft, gentle pleasure.

I would fight an entire platoon of Roths. I would move worlds for this small human.

Ni-Kee has my whole heart.

CHAPTER
TWENTY-SIX

NIKI

MY RECOVERY IS SLOWER than I would like. Three days since I woke up, we've been stuck here at the cave, waiting for me to be strong enough to leave.

"Keep going, my Ni-Kee," Draz encourages.

Sweat drips from my temples, and I move through the martial arts stances I learned decades ago, as a child, from my mother. My breath comes in great heaving gasps. It shouldn't be this hard, and impatience rips through me.

I sit down heavily, finishing the set, and press my chin to my knees.

Draz hands me a water canteen, and I drink it greedily.

"Your way of fighting is not so different from ours," he tells me. "You could help train our warriors, if you like."

I shrug, caught off guard. Rationally, I know that Sueva is my only option. But something about planning for the future makes me feel… weird. Draz is amazing, and it has nothing to do with him. In fact, sometimes, when he catches me staring at him, my heart squeezes so hard with affection it's nearly painful.

But I can't quite wrap my mind around my future here.

Maybe it's being stuck in this cave. Maybe it won't feel real until I can check on my crew and see how they're faring, make sure that they understand that the Federation will consider us persona non-grata if we return to Earth.

Thinking about the Federation opens up a dark, yawning hole deep inside me, but I shut it down, concentrating on the cool water on my tongue, the sweat sliding down my spine.

"What is wrong? Does your wound trouble you?" His voice is laced with concern.

"No. It feels better, thanks to you." I pause, trying to decide if I should tell him. I don't want to hurt his feelings.

"I can tell you are hurting," he says, a note of reproach in his tone.

When I look up at him, his eyes are narrowed, his tail twitching from side-to-side.

"I am hurting," I say slowly. "But not from that."

"Did I push you too hard?" His face is thunderous, his fangs showing.

"No, no, not at all. It's not physical." I sigh. I know him well enough now to know he won't stop asking, and there's no way around it.

"It is mental? You do not like being weak."

"I mean, that's true, yes, but this isn't anything compared to what I went through after taking that plas pulse to the hip from the Roth." I point to the scar, grimacing at the memory. "It took me a month to be able to walk, and about six until I was back to normal. It still hurts when it gets cold out."

"Then it is good that you will stay on Sueva, where it does not get very cold."

"That's true," I say, a flicker of distress moving over me.

"Is it me, then?" Draz's tail thrashes. "Have you changed your mind?"

"It's not you, not at all. I care for you. I just... I started thinking about my crew, and about how I am going to have to explain to them that the Federation has closed Earth to us, and it makes me worried for them. I am lucky, because you're the one who married me, and we get along really well. I'm worried that they aren't having the same luck, and I'm frustrated, because I'm stuck here until I'm well enough to leave, and I can't even check on them."

"I understand this frustration. Let me make something clear, though." He crouches down next to me, placing a hand over his heart. "I am the lucky one."

"Draz," I say, unable to stop the smile across my lips. He runs a taloned finger across my mouth, his gaze heating.

"I worry that my need for you is slowing your progress."

"Well, it's certainly stopping this conversation."

He lets out a bark of a laugh, rocking onto his heels and standing up, offering me a hand. "I think you are ready for the journey to Edrobaz. When you get tired, we will rest. If you are still too tired, I will carry you."

I cock my head. "Are you worried about the warlords and my crew, too?"

He nods once, a speculative look on his face. "I am not worried, not about that, no. But I am worried that not being with your crew is causing you much stress. I think that you need to see them for yourself before you will be able to move forward with me."

His unspoken words hang heavy between us. I squint at him, wondering if he's hinting around having babies again, but he just watches me carefully right back. He hasn't said a word about it since our conversation after he went fishing, and I trust that he would if he was truly bothered by it.

So maybe it's me, then, maybe it's all in my head, that I feel guilty and weird about telling him I'm not ready to have his children. Ugh. I'm tangled up inside.

Seeing my crew, talking this shit over with them, will help. He's right about that, at least. I frown, thinking over his words.

"You said you're not worried about that. There is something you're worried about? The separatists?" I guess.

"Bah. We can handle the separatists. Besides, the two we let go were quite taken with you. I would be surprised if the rest do not fall in line once word spreads of how desirable the human females are."

I dip my chin at him, one eyebrow raised.

"And how intelligent, brave, and ferocious you are," he adds belatedly, a hint of a smile on his face.

"And," I prompt, grinning.

"And perfect in every way," he says, his big hands circling my waist. His face falls, and he blows out a breath. "I am worried about something."

For Draz to be worried, this big, strong warlord, it must be serious, and tension stiffens my shoulders.

"What?"

"Have you heard that roaring, nearer to the cave today?"

"Yeah? I figured it was just something in the jungle."

"It is something in the jungle, and that is the problem. It should not be in the jungle. The Crigomar should stay to the southern swamps, but it is here, too near our Suevan cities and Edrobaz. We need to leave and warn them."

"What is a Crigomar, exactly?"

His talons bite into my skin, not enough to hurt, but enough to tell me he's stressed about them, whatever they are.

"They are a massive species. Carnivorous. Plated skin, fierce opponents. They are difficult to kill, and it is not something our people take lightly, to kill a Crigomar. They are important to our ecosystem, but the fact that they are out of their normal habitat is troubling indeed. There is also the small matter that they are a source of many legends for our people."

"Don't tell me they're like the sacred snails from hell."

He snorts, his fang flashing as he grins. "No. They are not sacred. Simply a cultural myth."

"How big are we talking?"

Draz turns his chin up, silently measuring the cave. "Twice as big as this space."

"Oh. Oh, wow. And you said scaled hide? Like, erm, a giant lizard?"

"Yes. They say we are their descendants, that we evolved from them."

"All right," I say. I'm not going to touch that one. It's still too weird to consider the truly alien parts of Draz's people. "They sound like dinosaurs."

"Dino-sawers?"

Clearly there is no translation available, and I grin at him. It's adorable when he tries to say English words.

"They went extinct on our planet millions of years ago." I shrug. "Big reptiles."

"Interesting," he says, his eyes glimmering.

A roar sounds from outside the cave, distant enough not to be an immediate threat, but a shiver runs down my spine nonetheless.

His gaze cuts to the entrance, all amusement disappearing. "We have about eight hours of daylight left. Do you think you could start our trek to Edrobaz now?"

Shock ripples through me. It's one thing to discuss returning, facing my crew and their... husbands, and it's something else entirely to start the hike there now.

"You must be pretty worried."

He dips his head in acknowledgment.

"You should have told me they were a threat before now."

"You're right," he agrees, not even bothering to say something stupid about how I needed rest or give another excuse.

Real fear trickles ice cold down my back, primal and raw, as the Crigomar call sounds again.

"Let's get our stuff together."

"I packed it while you slept this morning."

"Is that right?" I ask, real annoyance rearing its head. "And when were you going to tell me?"

"I wanted to see how your exercises went before I made a final call."

"My opinion should have been a part of your final call, Draz. You can't just make unilateral decisions without me. That's not going to work."

His lips thin, and for a moment, I wonder if he's going to argue.

"You're right. Forgive me, my heart. I am unused to asking for opinions. I am a Suevan Warlord. I was trained by blood and bone to make the decisions that are in my people's best interests."

"And I'm a captain in the Earth Federation. I can help make decisions with you. You don't have to bear them all on your own."

It hits me with crystal clarity, then. I could be a leader here, too. What the Earth Federation taught me carries as much weight here as it does there.

The dark abyss of worry inside me closes, just a little, at the thought.

I wrap my hands around his neck, smiling up at him and fluttering my eyelashes.

"Draz… have there ever been any female Suevan warlords?"

He barks out a laugh. "Of course, there have. You have such strange ideas about us, my mate."

Good.

I like that answer very much.

CHAPTER
TWENTY-SEVEN

DRAZ

NI-KEE'S BRAID bobs in front of me, her shoulder just ahead of mine. The jungle sings with life around us, the air growing thinner the further up the mountain we trek. Here, the foliage isn't as dense, but I keep my energy edged knife in hand.

A crossbow dangles from my mate's hand, and I am glad she knows how to use it.

I do not like how close the Crigomar are. It baffles me that they would leave their lands and follow the Suevans up into the higher elevations. It is unheard of.

Something must be driving them higher. Whether latent instinct or newly manufactured, I know not.

But I do know that we need to get to Edrobaz as quickly as we can. My heart yearns to show my mate the city, to let her marvel at the architecture and art, at all the fine things that await her here on Sueva.

It will be hard to show her that if the Crigomar continue to track us at the rate they are.

I have no proof that is what they are doing, not exactly... but I have a feeling.

And years on the battlefield has taught me to listen to that instinct, so on we press, higher and higher up the mountain, until each breath is sharp and cold.

"Do you need rest, my heart?"

She shakes her head, her long braid swinging. "No."

Her face is set with determination, and though worry claws through me, her eyes are clear and her breathing is steady.

"How much longer?"

I squint at the patch of sky overhead, the asteroid belt clearly visible against the deep blue. "A day. Maybe more, if I have taken us too far off course."

"Are we off course?"

"Not that I can tell."

"Okay, then," she says. "Let's get to it."

My heart swells. This woman is stronger than I ever would have imagined. As frail and delicate as her body is compared to mine, she has the heart and mind of a warrior twice her size.

"We can rest if you have the need, Ni-Kee," I offer softly.

"Nope. Don't need to. Tell me about your city. About Edrobaz."

I grin, reaching for her hand. When she squeezes mine back, satisfaction and pleasure roll through me.

"It is not as grand as some of the other cities, but I like it all the better for that. We are not a city of scientists, or even warriors, though we have both. We are a city of artists. There is much I cannot wait to show you."

"Artists? Really?"

"Yes. If we were Lidolan, we would likely have already been found by their technology. But Lidolan is a month away on foot, though only a day by Levoz."

"Levoz?"

"A ship. It sails through the skies, very quickly. I forget so easily how unfamiliar you are with Sueva. It's strange, considering how I feel you have slotted into my life like a piece that's been missing as long as I've breathed."

She squeezes my hand, and her smile is sunlight on my senses.

"You say the most romantic things."

"They are all true," I tell her.

She draws one arm around me, then presses her cheek against my chest, holding me tight.

"No one's ever made me feel like you do," she says softly, her voice the merest caress against my senses.

"Good," I say simply, kissing the top of her head. "I would have to kill them if you did."

She snorts, pushing against me with a laugh. "You're ridiculous."

I watch her for a moment, and she turns back, her eyebrows raised.

"You're serious."

"Of course, I am serious. I will not stand for a competitor for your attention."

"Okay then," she says, her voice strangled. "Glad we cleared that up."

Now curiosity winds through me. "Did you have many suitors on Earth?"

"No," she says fervently, her braid swinging in earnest now. "Definitely not."

"Then human males are even more foolish than I imagined." With a hand on the small of her back, I guide her slightly left, tracking closer to Edrobaz. "I find I am less and less impressed with the world you left behind."

Which makes me glad. How can she miss Earth when Sueva holds so many more opportunities for her? Surely her team will see reason, as well. And then we can negotiate for more brides, willing this time, until Edrobaz and Lidolan and all the cities run rampant with the sounds of children's feet and ring with their laughter.

I want that so badly. For myself, and for my people.

"Earth isn't perfect," she says softly, moving more quickly up the mountainside in the direction I pushed her in. "But it's my home."

I wince. That was poorly done.

Not that I am wrong, of course. Still, perhaps I should take a different tactic.

"Would you like to hear about my house?" I ask her. I cannot wait to see her in it, decked out in something more befitting a Suevan warlord's bride than the lackluster uniform she wears now. I cannot wait to see her sprawled in my bed, her legs spread and her sex glistening for me.

My cock grows hard at the vision, and I bite back a groan.

Will I ever have enough of this woman? I do not think so.

"I didn't have a house," she says instead, her fingers twitching on her crossbow. "I had an apartment with Gen, in the city. I loved it. We always joked that we didn't really live there, of course. As officers we could live off base, but we spent so much time on missions or at work that we were rarely there. But it was my space, and hers, and it was our sanctuary. I had a plant I got, too, one that wasn't supposed to need a lot of care, because I knew I wouldn't be able to give it too much time, until I got back. I had a new bedding set picked out, too, and I was going to reward myself with it and a bunch of candy when I got back from this mission. I guess my plant is probably going to die now." Her voice is heavy, and her shoulders droop.

"I will get you a new plant."

A heavy sigh gusts out of her. "Thank you. It's not about the plant."

"We can commission an artist to make whatever bedding you like," I tell her. "Anything you want, I will make it happen for you." I do not like how sad she sounds now, and it makes me feel helpless. Angry.

She still does not see the depth of my feelings for her. What wouldn't I do to show her?

Anything. *Anything*.

And she is right, I realize, whacking at a plant that dared

wave too close to her slender leg. Her crew and companions are likely even more obstinate and stressed than my sweet mate, especially if they have not bonded with their mates.

The sooner we get to Edrobaz, the better.

In the meantime, I will make my mate as comfortable as I can. I will pamper her and shower her with affection. Maybe I can even find some more of the can-dee berries she likes so much. That will bring a smile to her face, at least.

CHAPTER
TWENTY-EIGHT

NIKI

I'M NOT MYSELF. For all the resting I've done the last three days, on top of the four days I apparently spent completely passed out, my arms and legs feel like lead, my lungs like deflated balloons.

Worry creases Draz's handsome face, his forehead bunching every time I glance at him. The Crigomar roars are further now, but from this altitude, I can see the jungle canopy shake whenever one makes that monstrous sound.

Draz is one of the scariest badasses I've ever been around, and he doesn't want to fuck around with the creatures. We have state of the art alien tech—an energy knife and my crossbow fitted with plas grenade rounds— and he still doesn't want us anywhere near them.

A cold lump of fear forms in my throat, a wonderful accompaniment to the exhaustion weighing me down.

"You are still unwell," Draz says, stopping to look back at where I lag behind. My chest heaves.

"It's the altitude," I tell him. "My body isn't used to the oxygen levels up here."

"We're done for the day."

"How much farther is it? I can keep going."

"You are done for the day, my heart. I will not have you push yourself to exhaustion."

"How much further? I can make it." Maybe the lack of oxygen is making me cranky. Or maybe it's his bossiness.

He cranes his head up, checking our location against the asteroid belt above. "At least six hours."

"Fuck," I say, scrubbing a hand down my face.

"Right now?"

"No, for crying out loud—" I stop when I notice he's laughing at me, so handsome, with that big smile that my heart skips.

"I know, my heart, I am teasing you. Come. We will make camp early, and you can go to sleep while I get dinner together. I noticed a can-dee berry bush not too far back. I will go back for them now, and you will rest."

"Oh, yum, those berries do sound good." Something about what he's saying niggles at me, bothering me, but a yawn cracks my jaw, and he wraps me in a big hug.

I sag against him, soaking up the warmth of his scaled hide, the familiar and delicious way his hard chest feels against me.

"My sweet mate, you are so very tired. And so very stubborn."

I don't argue because he's damn right. I am both. He lets me go, and I sway where I stand, like suddenly not being in motion has made all the aches and pains and exhaustion even worse.

"Poor, beautiful mate." His voice is tender, and he sets up the blankets against a huge boulder. "Sit, sit."

I do as he says, and the face of the boulder is a welcome heat against my back.

"All right?"

"Yes, I'm okay." I swig from the water canteen, my eyelids sagging. "You're right though," I grudgingly admit. "I did need rest."

"I know," he says, a smug smile firmly placed.

I roll my eyes, laughing a little. The zoleh jumps into my lap, cuddling close. It's hard to believe this bold little thing is the same one that found me in the hollow tree a week and a half ago. It's filled out since it attached itself to me, and its fur has become glossy and fluffy.

I'm just glad the zoleh's stinky breath has improved.

I look up to find Draz watching me, a fond smile on his face. I grin up at him, then yawn again.

"Use the pack as a pillow, and dream of me. I will return in a moment and start a fire for us."

"That sounds nice," I say, and do as he says. Too tired to argue, and smart enough to at least realize my body still needs as much rest as it can get.

With the zoleh clutched in my arms, and the promise of food and fire, I fall asleep quickly.

———

I awake shivering. Stars burn cold overhead, the sky more readily visible from this height. It's cold.

There's no fire.

I sit bolt upright, trembling. The zoleh cracks three eyes, then hops off my lap, circling around its tails before curling up beside me.

"Draz?" I say softly.

My heart beats erratically, painfully.

He's not here. I glance around, but it's full night, and out here, that means it's dark as deep space.

I swallow hard, my breath sticking in my throat. Oh my God. He could be anywhere. He could be hurt.

I don't want my warlord to be hurt. *He could be worse than hurt.*

Real fear sluices over me, and I shiver.

"Zoleh," I say, poking the furry animal. "I need help. Draz is missing."

It raises its head, then settles back down. Right. The little thing acts so intelligent half the time, but expecting it to sit up and bark like a rescue dog is clearly a sign I'm losing my fucking mind. Perfect.

I have to find Draz.

The good thing is, I can do this. Search and rescue *was* part of my training, and while it's been a while, I'm confident that if he's hurt somewhere, I can find him and help him.

I squeeze my eyes shut, guilt swamping me. Why did I tell him I wanted the stupid fucking berries? I should have just told him to stay with me. What the fuck was I thinking?

"Fuck," I snarl, standing up, rooting through one of the packs. I shove a blanket in it in case he's got some kind of alien exposure issues. The length of rope and some of our dried troblek rations follow.

"I'm going to find you Draz," I say, determination pounding through me.

I never expected to marry a massive alien warlord, but he's mine now.

He won't get rid of me so easily.

CHAPTER
TWENTY-NINE

DRAZ

MY HEAD RINGS, and the blindfold around my eyes blunts my vision. The traitors have gone far enough to gag me.

"I can scent the human on him," one says, speaking guttural, accented Suevan.

My suspicions were right then. With that accent, this group of separatists are from the swamplands, and they likely drove the Crigomar further into our territory to sow chaos and discord.

"She smells good," another answers, and I thrash against the bonds tying my hands and feet. "They said she was beautiful too, for an alien. Soft and round."

Underpopulation be damned, I am going to kill them all at the first chance I get. If I don't, my fierce Ni-Kee will be in danger. I will not allow her to fall into their foul hands.

Shame winds through me. I never should have left her alone. I should have stayed with her. They should not have been able to sneak up on me, like the disgusting cowards they are, to knock me out from behind while I stooped to gather her beloved can-dee berries.

The bonds hold tight though, the ropes knotted in the correct way, the way we all learn as children.

"He is taken with her," a new voice says, my translator processing the words. "They are a mated couple?"

My scales tremble at the memory this new voice stirs, and my tail goes still. That is not a Suevan voice.

"The others said that they weren't when they found them, though she fought like a Crigomar to help him. I am curious what the human female looks like. Maybe we can go and find her for ourselves."

A wordless roar tumbles from my mouth. I will murder them if they so much as think about my mate.

"Definitely a mated pair," the slick, foreign voice muses, and I can hear the avid interest in it. "And you said the humans are compatible with your species? You can procreate with them?"

"That is what the researchers said," the Suevan traitor replies. He must have intel from Lidolan. The separatists must have an asset in place there. When I get out of here, I will order a sweep.

We must remove this rotten branch, and quickly.

"Fascinating," that cold voice says, closer now.

Come here, so I can strike you with my talons, old foe.

The Roth.

I would kill him for what his people did to my mate alone. Not to mention what his species did to her homeworld and dozens of our settlements. Death and destruction follow the Roth. There's no negotiating with them. They are a conquering species, a species who devours.

The worst kind.

My lip curls in a snarl, and I strain against the well-tied bonds.

What has he promised the southern separatists, to goad them into this?

"Look how the warlord struggles. Draz, Draz, Draz, after what you did to my brother in the wars, tossing his spine out like so much trash, you should be thankful I haven't pulled your intestines through your nose."

Someone shifts, and there's an uncertainty to it that I hone in on immediately—the way the Suevan tail lashes signals many different things, something this Roth no doubt is clueless about.

This Suevan's tail is telegraphing unease. Whether it's with the Roth's threat or having me in his camp, I do not know.

But uncertainty is a poor trait in a soldier, and one I can no doubt capitalize on.

"What was it like, to degrade yourself by fucking a human female? Was it like screwing a beast?"

I growl, knowing he's trying to enrage me, knowing it and incensed all the same.

The Roth laughs, a low, guttural sound. "They are a primitive species. You should see what they've done to their atmosphere, to their native flora and fauna. Atrocious. Truly, I could not believe it when I heard the mighty Sueva was treatying with them, offering them advanced technology."

Something large crashes through the bush behind me, and a roar follows. A Crigomar and too close for comfort.

"Get it under control," the Roth hisses, and taloned feet dig into the jungle soil, maybe three Suevans at most. "We need the element of surprise. They can't know we've brought them. How many times do I have to explain it to you?"

The element of surprise.

He means to take it to Edrobaz, the only populated city on this mountain.

He means to destroy my home.

Fear trickles over me, but I push it down. I will find a way out of this. I must.

"You there, yes you."

A Suevan tail thwaps against the ground.

"You go find the female. Bring her back to camp. He'll tell us everything once we have her. Do you know the funny thing about humans, friend? They're soft, and so easy to make scream."

The cords cut into my wrists, my biceps. I won't allow it. I will not allow them to hurt my Ni-Kee. I let out a deep, warning growl, hissing at the end.

"See? He's practically proving it now."

I will pull the bones from the Roth's flesh slowly. Meticulously.

"What if she puts up a fight?" the separatist Suevan asks, moving carefully around the campsite.

"She is human." A snort of derision. "They only think they can put up a fight."

The Suevan's tail lashes against the forest floor. "That's not what the ones who saw her said. They said she was a fighter, a warrior. And that she was fair of face and body."

I snarl, unable to contain myself, unable to break free, unable to help my sweet, sleeping Ni-Kee.

When she is awake, she is stubborn and fierce, every inch the warrior the separatists call her. But my mate is asleep, and ill, and all too fragile.

I never should have left her alone.

CHAPTER
THIRTY

NIKI

I WISH I could see in the dark. It's fucking ridiculous how hard it is to see at night. Lucky Draz with his stupid Suevan vision shouldn't have any problems, but me?

Fucking stupid human eyeballs.

My irritation fuels me, though, and I keep looking for signs of him, moving quietly as I can through the vegetation.

There.

A berry bush. My breath catches as I lean closer, the cloud cover parting momentarily, allowing a sliver of moon to flash against something long and metal.

I sink to my knees, feeling like I've been punched in the gut.

Draz's energy knife.

There's no blood on it, it's clean… I squint, cursing my lack of night vision, as the moonlight flickers overhead, scanning the area for any signs of what happened to him, any signs of a predator or…

Oh no.

There are blood spatters against a large branch, not more than three feet away.

What the fuck?

Did he hit his head and then wander off?

"I do not like how he talks to me," a voice mutters.

My adrenaline kicks into overdrive, and I crouch, backing up into the berry bush, the knife in one hand and my crossbow in the other.

"Go get her. Bring her back." It's said in a different voice, like the Suevan's doing a poor impression of someone else. Whoever's in charge, probably. " Like we're his pets, fetching the human to get him to talk. Besides, I like the way her scent smells on him. These humans cannot be so bad if Draz, the first warlord, wants one."

There's a grunt in response to this, and I cringe.

The human?

Get him to talk?

These motherfuckers took Draz. My eyes slide to the fallen branch. They hit him over the head, and took him somewhere else, to try and pump information out of him. And they're going to use me to do it.

Fuck that.

My adrenaline and rage mingle, a heady combination. All my training and expertise kickstarts my brain, and a million different plans take shape in my head. The zoleh's eyes are wide in the dim light, reflecting it back at me eight times.

There's two Suevans, and one me, and one alien pet who may or may not be any help. I need to find where they took Draz, and considering I can't see shit at night, I need them to show me there.

The question is, what's the right lever to pull?

Force? Fear?

Something else?

Fuck. I wish our crew's xenobiologist had given us more intel about this species. I'm limited to what Draz has told me about this planet, about his people, and what I've garnered from living with him and falling in love with him.

Falling in love with him.

My heart stutters, then stops, before pounding even more furiously.

I love him.

If they've hurt him, I'm going to go absolutely feral. One hundred percent murder robot mode.

"Do you smell that?" one Suevan asks. "I think we must be close to the human female."

"She smells very good," the other Suevan says plaintively. There's a wistful quality in his voice, and the plan comes to me.

Foolhardy, idiotic, even, but the odds of me physically overwhelming the two of them are slim to none.

I've always told Gen you catch more flies with honey than vinegar.

I guess it's time to put that cliché to the test.

The crossbow clips to my side, and I tug the strap of my tank down, taking the time to push my boobs up as far as they'll go. It's not much, because sports bras aren't exactly the sexiest, but considering how much Draz is obsessed with them, I figure a little goes a long way.

"Oh my goodness," I say, stumbling out of the berry bush. Sure, I have two seriously powerful weapons in my hand, but these Suevans already underestimate me, so I do my best to look small and helpless.

My lashes flutter extra hard for good measure.

The Suevans stop, staring at me with wide eyes, the moonlight glinting off their scales.

I consider throwing out a 'hello, boys,' but clamp my lips shut to keep the words from coming out.

"I am so glad you found me," I say. Their surprised faces would be almost comedic, were it not for the fact that my warlord is somewhere, out there in the jungle, hurt or worse.

Not worse. Can't be. I won't let it happen.

"You are the human female?" one says, stepping closer, his big tail twitching behind him.

Ah yes, there's that trusting Suevan sensibility, they're proclivities not to lie making this a helluva lot easier than it would be on Earth.

"Definitely. I need your help, you see? Draz, that's my mate, you know, he was telling me that his warriors would be out here shortly—"

One of the Suevans makes a surprised grunt, standing up taller and looking around.

I clear my throat, rolling my shoulders back. *Focus, you horny lizardmen.* Never thought I'd be playing the part of the honey trap, but desperate times…

"You must be the ones he was talking about, right? The ones that I'm going to call back to Earth and tell them we need more women for? More human women?" I blink rapidly, grinning at them. My heart's slamming against my ribs, and I'm lying so hard I'm surprised my nose isn't going full Pinocchio.

"Draz is requesting more women from Earth?" one rasps, stepping closer.

"Yes, of course he is. We have so many women there, and they are all so—" I pause, stumbling over the lie. "Excited to find a husband. They love to mate. Yep. They especially want a husband as fierce and, ah, big as the Suevans. But the problem is, Draz is gone. I don't know what happened to him, but he can't send the comm to Earth for more human women now, since he's gone."

Take the bait. Take the bait.

"She does not seem very fierce," one says to the other, and the other shushes him with a violent hiss.

"She smells good," he adds, and I keep my cringe at bay. I do not want either of these scaly oafs sniffing at me.

"All human women smell like me." I'm laying it on pretty thick, but what else am I supposed to do? As much confidence as I have in my fighting skills, I'm not Gen. And I'm not at my full strength, something I would definitely need to be able to take down two full-grown Suevans.

"They do?" one asks hopefully.

"Can you help me find Draz?" I say, making my voice small. I want to scream at them, and it takes all my self-control to swallow it. "Do you know where he is?"

"You like Draz? He is not displeasing to you?"

"I love him." It's the first time I haven't lied, and the words are so true they hurt, slicing me open from the inside out.

They look at each other, clearly trying to make up their minds about what to do.

"I want the best for my people, and from what I can tell, the Suevans are our best choice." That tumbles out of me, catching me by surprise. It's true, too—though I don't mean all human women, just my crew.

The Suevans *are* our best choice, and I need Draz at my side to present the facts to them. I need him.

"Please take me to him," I say, my throat closing up with emotion.

"The Roth—" one starts to say, but the other silences him with a sharp elbow to the side.

My insides go cold. A Roth? Why would he bring up a Roth?

"We will take you to him," the bigger of the two says.

"He will be so grateful to see me," I reply. Worry threads through me, my internal alarm bells sounding loudly. "I am sure he will reward you both."

A firm hand closes over my bicep, and fear slices across my senses. What if I've misjudged the situation? These two... they are separatists. They're the same group that blew up my ship and the peaceful Suevan mating ceremony. Maybe they don't have the same idea of honor that my Draz does.

Shit.

I let my eyes close briefly. I could have followed them, or at least tried to, or done any number of other equally dangerous things. But I made a split-second decision, and now I have to see how it plays out.

"So… there are many like you?" one of them says, tugging me along behind.

"There are eight in my crew, but we're all different, just like you are. But there are many, many women on Earth. And I'm sure they will be lining up to come here once I tell them how wonderful Sueva is, and how handsome the Suevans are." I'm babbling, the words tripping over themselves with my need to make him think I'm too important to hand over.

Lie, lie, lie.

The one in front grunts, his tail thrashing back and forth. It nearly whacks against my shin, but I step back at just the right moment to avoid it. He's agitated, but I don't know if it's because of me, or what I'm saying, or because the goddamned Roth they mentioned.

"That's why they sent me," I continue, my tone chirpy and light, like we're on a stroll through the park and not at all like I'm being tugged along a jungle path by two separatists that may or may not have blown up my goddamned ship.

"You are important on Earth."

"Of course, I am. That's why they entrusted this mission to me, you know? I'm a high-ranking Federation officer, and they will believe me when I tell them what awaits here in Sueva."

"I cannot believe you human women survived the virus."

"Virus?" I ask sweetly, with the tone of someone inquiring about the weather. Laying it on a little thick, maybe, but I'm in too fucking deep now.

"The contagion that mutated our genome and made it impossible to conceive females. The Roth suffer from it, too."

"It's why they invaded your planet," the one in front adds blithely, and familiar fear and fury strangle me. "They were looking for a cure."

"They murdered thousands of innocent people," I spit, all simple syrupy sweetness gone from my voice, evaporated and leaving behind only crystallized rage. "They weren't after species continuation. They were after extinction."

I never thought I was a particularly violent person before the Roth. Now, the mere mention of them sends my blood boiling.

"That is how the Roth operate," the one holding me says. "They do not think like we do. It is simply their way."

I need to get a grip on myself.

"You are right," the one in front says, turning to the Suevan at my side. "What you said is right. They do not act with honor. They do not consider other species to be worthy of them."

They gape at each other for a moment, as though they've just put something together.

"We need to protect this human," the one in front says suddenly. "She will bring more mates from her world. Willing human mates."

"The Roth…" the one holding me squeezes my arm, his talons biting into my flesh. I wince, trying to use the pain to center my thoughts, to dull the worry. "He will be displeased."

"He is using us," the one with brains says, and my stomach flops.

There is a Roth here.

"A Roth has Draz," I grit out, the words like gravel in my throat. "I will fucking kill him." My hip aches with the phantom memory of that plas pulse I took, all those years ago.

And now one has my mate?

Dead alien walking.

"She *is* fierce," the one holding me says, his eyes blinking so slowly, I'm half-concerned his third eyelids' stuck. "The human women are fierce like you?"

"We're a bunch of grade A bitches," I tell him, my teeth grinding together in impatience. "We need to get to your camp and get Draz. He will help you. He doesn't want to hurt any Suevans, he wants your people to thrive."

"Which is why he secured you as his mate," one says knowingly. "Perhaps we have made an error in judgment by listening to the Roth. Human females are not weak or ugly."

"Ah, thank you." I scrunch my nose. "We need to move. *Now.*"

The Suevans both look at me curiously, and I realize I've used my no-nonsense command tone.

"I have a plan," I add.

And if it doesn't work, I might just get us all killed.

Fun fun fun.

CHAPTER
THIRTY-ONE

DRAZ

MY CHIN HANGS against my chest, my limbs heavy at my sides. I am not asleep, but I am as close to it as I can get. I must conserve my strength.

I will need all of it to eviscerate my old foe.

The sound of feet approaching jerks me from my reverie, but I stay still, breathing slowly, flooding my lungs with oxygen.

I inhale deeply and nearly choke on a familiar, tantalizing scent.

Ni-Kee.

No.

Still, I do not move, do not give away the dark depths of my worry, the wild need to put myself between her and the Roth.

"We found the human female," one of the traitor Suevans says, and my mate gives a small whimper. My blood runs cold, and my lip curls from my fangs. "She is a weak and ugly thing, just like you said she would be."

"So ugly," another Suevan says, and confusion overshadows my worry.

Ni-Kee is not ugly. Strange, maybe, with her smooth skin and odd green and gold eyes, but decidedly beautiful in spite of it. Not even Prince Kanuz was disappointed by the females. In fact, the picky prince was thrilled with the selection.

"Please, don't hurt me," Ni-Kee says, and all thoughts flee my mind, replaced by a furious need to deal as much damage to the Roth and my traitorous brethren as possible.

I grunt, struggling against the bonds yet again, only succeeding in driving them deeper into my arms.

"Stand up, human female, so that I may look upon you." The Roth's curious and cruel voice makes my stomach clench. "They say that you are breedable. Is that correct?"

Ni-Kee sniffles, and I know she is making the eye-water again. Out of fear. I am going to crack his bones and shove them up his—

"Yes, I am very fertile. I have always wanted children, just like all human women."

I stop struggling, astounded. Is this true? This cannot be true. I wish I could see her face, I wish I could tell her to stop talking. Doesn't she know the Roth were hit first and hardest by the virus? That they are all but extinct and desperate in the face of their species' mortality?

He's here for the humans.

The knowledge sears through me, and I redouble my efforts.

The Roth have come to take our human females.

"That is very good." He sighs. "You know, it is a pity you are mated to this scaled male. I could give you much more than this backwater swamp of a planet."

"Oh?" Ni-Kee says, her voice heated and low.

I growl, unable to stop myself. That is my woman. She said she cared for me. Why would she use that voice for him? That is a voice for my ears alone.

"You know, humans do not mate. Not like, ah, many other species seem to."

Footsteps sound, and I hear Ni-Kee suck in a breath.

What is he doing to her?

This is torture.

"Are you offering to come with me?" the Roth says, amused, and my stomach turns to fire, my heart igniting with the fury of a burning sun. "What a fickle bunch of cowards you humans are."

"Let the warlord go," she says softly, and I can hear the sultry smile on her lips. "Let him go, and you can have me. Easy as that."

Too late, I realize what she's doing.

And there is nothing I can do to stop the stubborn woman.

CHAPTER
THIRTY-TWO

NIKI

THE ROTH AREN'T horrible looking. There's no scales, no tentacles, no strange appendages that set so many alien species far apart from humanity. His skin is dark grey, mottled black spirals curling all over his bare chest, and his hair hangs long, all the way down his back. His full-black eyes are cold and merciless. I school my face into vapid expressionless, trying not to show anything but idiocy as I blink up at him. The Roth are huge, bigger than the Suevans even, with tough, leathery hide. It's easier to slice through, though. I grin at the memory, then press my lips into a thin line.

My memories didn't exaggerate the size difference.

The Suevans still hold my arms, as though they captured me and brought me here, before this motherfucker.

My elbows are drawn up high, like uncomfortable chicken wings, and my palms sweat against the energy knife tight in my hands, hidden behind my back.

I just need him to come closer.

"Let the warlord go?" the Roth repeats. "You just offered

yourself to me. Your body and future children to me. Why do you care what happens to this scum?"

"Why do you?" I counter. "Aren't you here for the women? What does he have to do with it?"

His eyes are wide with incredulity and full of contempt. "No wonder your planet was so easy to infiltrate. Your intellect is staggeringly underdeveloped. I do not want the Suevans to come after the Roth. No one can know I was here, fool."

The Suevans pretending to hold my arms bristle next to me, and I pray that they'll stick to my stupid plan, that they'll fucking *listen*. The asshole just said he's going to kill them all once he's gotten his way.

Maybe I need to make it even clearer for them.

"You don't feel bad about killing even these guys? They've helped you." I want to check on Draz so badly, but there's no way to communicate my intentions to him. His eyes are blindfolded, his mouth gagged, and he's bound so tightly blood trickles bright in the silver moonlight from his wrists and biceps.

"You have a soft heart, do you not, female human? You worry about these Suevans lives? I wonder, will your body be as soft? Will you make soft, low noises when I'm inside you, planting my children?"

Draz makes a violent noise, and I barely keep from glancing at him. Planting? Why all the seed and plant imagery? Fucking aliens.

The Roth takes another step closer, and I work hard, so hard, not to telegraph my intention.

"If that's what you want," I tell the Roth, my heart racing so hard I'm dizzy. I need to calm down. I need to collect myself. I have to time this exactly right or we're all fucked.

Some of us more literally than others.

His black eyes burn into me, and fear jolts me at the red sparking in them. But it must be a trick of the light, because it quickly fizzles. Weird.

"I like this idea," the Roth says, his voice scraping over my already raw nerves.

He jerks his head at one of the Suevans holding me. "Take the warlord's blindfold off so that he may see me with his woman."

Oh, God. My heart cracks, and the remaining Suevan has the good sense to move behind me, holding my biceps up and helping maintain the illusion that I am helpless... and unarmed.

The Suevan moves to Draz slowly, and I lick my lips, my throat dry.

The blindfold falls away from Draz's eyes, and his gaze fixes on me immediately. The Suevan steps behind him. My heart flops painfully in my chest at the hurt etched across his brutally handsome features. The fear.

I love you. I want to scream it at him.

I don't dare move.

The Roth tsks at me, running a finger down my cheekbone and forcing my attention back to his dark grey face.

"You do not need to look at him," he says. "He needs to look at us."

The Roth moves even closer, so close that his chest brushes against mine, unspeakably and impossibly hot, so hot it nearly scorches through my tank.

I flinch.

Draz makes another strangled, tortured noise, his tail crashing behind him.

I blink up at him demurely.

He leans forward slowly, his fingers digging into my chin. His nostrils flare as he brushes his nose against my hair, inhaling deeply.

My skin crawls. Draz makes horrible growling noises, his tail thumping against the ground.

The Roth lowers his face to mine, and I keep my eyes open wide, letting some of my fear show.

"You will get used to it," the Roth says, towering over me. "My heat, that is."

"You won't get used to this," I say, and the Suevan behind me releases my arms, allowing me to plunge the energy knife into the Roth.

CHAPTER
THIRTY-THREE

DRAZ

I AM INCANDESCENT WITH RAGE. I am going to rip into the Roth with my talons, with my teeth. I am going to make him regret every breath he's ever drawn. I am going to watch as his blood bubbles from his mouth.

Ni-Kee… my Ni-Kee, reeks with the scent of her fear, and I know not what she has planned, but I know this is not her.

She is not the quiet, subservient woman she presents to the Roth.

She is playing at something, and I hate it. I hate that she must act thus, to distract him or to risk his wrath.

My stomach churns, sick with shame and desperation.

When he lowers his face to hers, inhaling her lovely human scent, I can bear it no longer. Hot blood streams from the wounds on my arms and wrists, and still I struggle, refusing to simply watch him move his body any closer to hers.

The threat of his lips meeting her mouth grows too real, and I'm snarling, beyond thought.

When she slips the knife—my energy knife—between his ribs, I almost don't notice it.

But the Roth stumbles back, his mouth opening and closing soundlessly.

It's not a killing blow, not necessarily for a Roth, but it's enough.

"She is as fierce as they said," one of the traitors says, and then his talons slice through my bonds. "You will bring us mates from her planet," he tells me.

I ignore him, launching myself at the Roth, putting myself between him and my mate.

Nothing will come between us again.

My talons jut into the leathery hide of the Roth, just below his chin. It would be so easy to end this, to end him.

He laughs wetly.

"Draz," Ni-Kee is saying, her soft hands on my shoulders. "Are you all right?" The question comes out on a choked sob, and I rub my tail across her leg, refusing to turn from the threat of the Roth.

"I should kill you slowly," I tell him.

"Do it," my mate says harshly from behind me. Fury radiates from every inch of her.

"Go ahead, then, Suevan warlord," the Roth says. He grins up at me, his teeth and fangs stained with blood. "Your female would have been mine. I would have replaced her memories of you with better ones of me. Humans are fickle. But now my people will know their women can be bred. And we will take them, by the hundreds, until the Roth are strong again."

"Bastard," Ni-Kee breathes.

Frustration sets me to snarling again, and I rake my talons across his throat, leaving new gashes there.

Not enough to kill him.

"We need him alive," I grit out. The other Suevans, the ones who Ni-Kee somehow managed to convince to help her, watch the proceedings with wary eyes.

"I think we'll be okay if he doesn't survive," Ni-kee says, and there's a bloodthirsty glint in her eyes that makes my blood sing.

The Roth laughs at this, his gaze skating over her skin.

"He's trying to goad us into killing him," I tell her.

I glance back at her, partly to reassure myself that she's alive and unhurt, and partly because I will never be able to go more than a few minutes without feasting my eyes on her again.

Her knuckles are white, a fist clenched so hard around the hilt of the energy knife that it trembles.

"I know that, and I'm tempted to do it all the same."

"Then do it if you can, human," the Roth taunts. "I will send word to every Roth ship in the galaxy that your planet is ripe for the picking. Human wombs will overflow with Roth offspring—"

Crack.

My elbow flies, landing squarely against his temple, and the Roth goes silent beneath me.

"Think, my love, think. Why would he be so desperate to end his own life? He knows something he does not want us to find out. He knows we can find it out. And so we take him back to Edrobaz, where we can persuade him to share what it is he so fervently does not want us know."

"Fuck." The word explodes out of her, the tension draining from her body. "We have to get the Federation that interplanetary defense system, and fast. What if he sent word back already? We can't allow the Roth to take my people."

I notice then how pale she is, how deep the circles beneath her eyes are.

"We honored our promise to send aid, my heart. A ship left from Lidolan with the tech as soon as the mating ritual began. It will be there quickly." I make a mental note to check on the ship's progress. Perhaps they should take a different route to Earth, to ensure that the tech arrives before any possible Roth ships closer to Earth.

"We will protect Earth as best we can. You and me, my human warrior."

"Why not a warlord?" she asks, and I grin at her.

"Is that what you want? To become a warlord? It is not enough to be married to one?" I already know her answer, but I want her to say it.

"Yes, and why not both?"

I stare at her for a long moment, before breaking into a smile. By the sky and Suevan ground, I am glad to see my female again.

"The Suevans helped me. The separatists." She jerks her chin at where the two Suevans still stare between us with uncertain eyes.

"They will be rewarded. Brothers, help me secure the prisoner."

The Roth's breathing is shallow and uneven. Every rational part of me knows that I should make sure he makes it to Edrobaz in one piece.

I still hope he dies painfully on the way.

The separatists toss me a length of rope, and I tie him quickly, not taking any care to be gentle.

Once I'm satisfied that he will not be able to wriggle free, I place a gag over his mouth. He's spread enough poison already.

"She said that you were negotiating for more human females from Earth," one of the southern Suevans said. "Your mate said that we would be allowed women of our own."

Incredulous, I slowly take in my clever, devious mate, who meets my gaze without a shred of shame.

She would do it all again. The truth of it's written across every defiant line of her face, in the stubborn set of her jaws and the lush pout of her mouth. This reckless, brave, and stubborn female risked herself to save me, and I'm equal parts furious with her and so very proud of her.

"Mine," I growl, then pull her close. She melts into me, and I cup her chin. My fangs scrape across her lips in a savage kiss, and the addictive scent of her arousal fans my lust higher.

I force myself to pull away, leaving Ni-Kee panting against

my chest, her fingers clutched against my back, as though she cannot stand to let me go.

My heart.

"We make for Edrobaz immediately," I tell the Suevans. "We will pull the Roth behind us on a sled. You will be welcome in my city for as long as you wish to stay."

A horrible roar goes up behind us, and icy fear skates over my senses.

The fucking Crigomar.

The separatists share a look, shifting uncomfortably as they note my obvious rage.

"Are they under control?"

"The Crigomar?" Ni-Kee asks.

"They're gaining ground," I tell her. "I swear to the Suevan skies, I will do all in my power to repair the bond between our people, but if the Crigomar hurt my mate or my people, you will wish you'd never been born."

The separatists exchange another nervous glance, their tails twitching behind them in tandem. "We understand."

"One of you needs to come with me, and the other needs to tell the rest of your team to turn back with the Crigomar." The words ring with the steel of command, and they stand up a little straighter.

"Understood." The taller of the two only hesitates momentarily. "Will I still be welcome in Edrobaz if I do not accompany you?"

"All Suevans are welcome in Edrobaz. But yes, I will tell my warriors to keep a lookout for you. Tell me your name, warrior."

"Gerzun and Idiz," he motions to his companion.

I bow my head to them, pounding a fist against my chest. "Go well with Sueva. We have much to mend. I look forward to reestablishing trust between our regions."

They echo the gesture. I may not trust the separatists, but they are Suevan. They helped my mate, and for that, I will be forever in their gratitude.

Gerzun snaps a limb off a nearby zitsu tree, lashing together a sled with practiced efficiency.

"A travois," my mate says. "Fascinating."

"The sled?" I say, not understanding the word she used.

"Yes. I bet Carmen is having the best time here."

"Carmen?" I tilt my head, trying to follow my mate's thoughts and failing.

"My xenobiologist. Our science officer." Ni-Kee scrubs a hand down her face before smiling brightly at me. "I am excited to see my crew."

"I am looking forward to meeting them." I rub a hand down her back, trying to shove down all my possessive, predatory instincts that scream at me to take her right now, to mate her and stamp her more firmly with my scent, signaling to anyone who approaches her that she is mine. "I am looking forward to showing you Edrobaz. And our home. And our mating room."

Her lips quirk upward in a smile. "Mating room?"

"Oh, yes, my heart." My cock grows stiff with the thought of her spread across my bed.

"Then we better hurry back."

I growl my approval.

The sooner we get back to Edrobaz, the sooner I can hear the sweet sounds my Ni-Kee makes as I bring her pleasure. The sooner I can bury myself in her and wash away the stink of the Roth from her skin and mind.

The Roth stirs on the sled, his wounds already healing, thanks to their biology, and I strike him sharply again.

He sags against his bonds, and satisfaction rolls through me.

"Let's go home," my Ni-Kee says, holding my hand like she's afraid it will disappear. I bring her knuckles to my lips, pressing a kiss there.

Home never sounded so sweet.

CHAPTER
THIRTY-FOUR

NIKI

EDROBAZ SPRAWLS BEFORE US, a bustling city unlike anything I've ever seen. It's in perfect harmony with the cloud-top jungle all around it, a meld of technology and nature that leaves me breathless. The city sits just above the cloud line, and the moisture licks at my ankles as we walk, giving the whole place an ethereal, unreal quality. Even without the curling mist, it would still be remarkable.

The trees here are impossibly huge, larger than the skyscrapers at home, towering further than I can see into the clear, blue sky. The air is crisp and clean, faintly pine scented, along with a bevy of other smells that my nose can't pick out. Archways glitter between them, sky bridges that link the glossy trunks. Small aircraft dart between buildings, silvery, shimmery shapes that defy any Earth laws of aerodynamics. Glass-like windows reflect sunlight in rainbow prisms, casting colorful light across the street.

"Wow." It's a feast for the senses, and my brain is over-whelmed.

"Do you like it?" Draz asks, his hand firm at my waist.

"It's incredible," I say honestly. This is my home now.

A few Suevans bustle through the streets, stopping to gape at the three of us, the Roth in tow, at the ornate gates.

"First Warlord Draz," a Suevan warrior calls out. "Welcome home. We sent out two search parties for you. It warms my scales to see you again."

The warrior's eyes glance over me, widening slightly as he takes in my disheveled appearance.

"Captain Jacks," he says, bowing his head and thumping his fist against his side in a gesture of respect. "Your crew will be overjoyed to see you have returned."

"Did they all make it? Are they all here?" Exhaustion melts away, leaving behind stony resolve. I need to see them immediately, to do my duty as their superior officer and break the news about how poorly we'd be received on Earth if any of them were to leave Sueva.

"Six of your people are here."

My heart stops. "Who is missing?"

"I do not remember her name. Apologies, Captain Jacks."

"Fuck," I mutter, and Draz squeezes my hand.

"Take the Roth to the prison cells under the warrior training grounds," Draz tells the warrior, who nods brusquely. "Follow tier nine protocols."

"Understood, Warlord." The warrior dips his chin in acknowledgment, slamming his fist against his side again.

"Order a guest suite prepared for our southern friends. We have much diplomacy to discuss."

The warrior beats his fist once more, his tail swishing and eyes narrowed at the former separatist.

"Follow me with the prisoner," he tells Gerzun. "I will send word of you and the Captain's arrival," the warrior adds.

My mind's tripping over the names and faces of my crew, working overtime in trying to decide who could still be out there in the steamy, dangerous Suevan jungle. Carmen, our scientist, or Tati, our medic, would be the most vulnerable. We're all trained in every discipline, but while Tati and Carmen are profi-cient in the skills required of Federation officers, neither have the same aptitude for survival as the rest of us.

I swallow hard, adrenaline sending a wave of nervous energy through me.

"Come, my heart," Draz says, pulling me close to him. "We will find them. They have two search teams out combing the jungles already. Whoever it is has a Suevan warlord with them. They will be safe."

"It is my job to keep them safe," I grit out. "I've failed them."

"You need rest. I have pushed you too hard the last few days."

"I need to see my crew, Draz. Don't manhandle me."

His hands slide over my waist, down to my hips, and lower still. "I do not know this word, man handle. But I do enjoy handling you."

I can't help the tiny smile on my lips. "I'm so glad you're all right, Draz."

"Come, come. Let us at least see you clean and check your wounds before you see them. You will only cause them stress if they see you in this state. They are safe for now, and everything possible is being done to see your missing member safe, too. Take care of yourself so that you may better take care of them."

I scuff my boot against the ground, annoyed that he's right. "Fine."

"Ah, my stubborn, beautiful mate, I love when you give in to me." His tone drips with sensuality, and heat rushes through me. "I think you like it, too."

I raise a finger up, scrunching my nose. "Clean clothes, food, and crew. In that order."

He does his best Suevan approximation of a pout, and I brush my fingertips across his jaw. "Why am I not on this list?"

"Why?" I ask, batting my eyelashes, knowing I'm playing with fire. "Did you want to come first?"

"Ni-Kee," he growls, his talons digging into my hips as he

pulls me flush against his chest. "You are lucky I am a patient male. Otherwise I would strip your pants from you and take you now, in front of all of Edrobaz."

My body clenches up as my eyes go wide in surprise. "You wouldn't."

"I would." He sniffs me delicately. "And I think you would like it."

I swallow hard. "Bath, clothes, food, crew... and then we can discuss the things I like." I grind into his cock. "At length."

"I like this new plan," Draz tells me. "Let's go home."

When he hooks his arm under my legs, another under my chest, I don't fight him. I melt into him instead, wrapping my arms around his neck and sighing contentedly.

I'll have to be Captain Jacks soon enough.

For now? I'm going to enjoy being his.

I can tackle everything else after.

CHAPTER
THIRTY-FIVE

DRAZ

THERE ARE TOO many things to see to. As soon as we enter my home, my staff rushes us, a million questions on their lips and in their eyes. The zoleh leaps from Ni-Kee's shoulders in alarm, scurrying up to a high shelf and hiding behind its tails.

"Later," I tell them. "Bring clothes for my mate and prepare a feast for her. My human needs me."

They nod, slamming their fists against their sides before scattering.

Ni-kee's eyes are huge in her face, their luminous green heart-shatteringly beautiful.

I cast a critical gaze over my home. It occupies the topmost quarters of the myza, our tree-top home, closest to the warrior training grounds, a traditional place for the warlord of Edrobaz. The spicy smell of the bark comforts me, as does the familiar, sprawling cylindrical shape.

But will she like it?

If she does not, she can pick whatever home she likes. Even if it is on the ground. Perhaps humans do not like to be so high in the air.

"What do you think?" I scratch my chin, the words gruff.

"I have never seen anything like this." Her voice is full of wonder, quiet and awed.

"Will you make it your home, my love?"

"Draz." Her gaze finds mine, and she steps into my embrace. "You're my home now. Where we live doesn't matter."

My heart stutters, and I hardly believe the words from her mouth. It is one thing to accept me as her mate when I am deep inside her, when she is overcome with sensation, or to even admit she is mine later.

"Draz, don't be so surprised. I love you," she says, blinking up at me, her heart shining in her expressive human eyes.

"My heart," I croak, sweeping her up into my arms. "You are the force I will navigate my life by. I will no longer look to the asteroids overhead for direction. My direction does not lie in the sky and the space above, but with you. You hold all of me in your small, human hands."

Her legs wrap around my waist, and she opens her mouth as I press a savage kiss against it. Desire rises in me, a hot, living thing, as her soft human tongue slides against a fang.

"Bath," she manages, clasping my face in her hands. "I have to check on my crew."

I grunt, annoyance flaring in me, along with pride. My Ni-Kee.

"You are a good leader," I tell her. "Even if I selfishly wish you were not."

"If you had your way, I would be screwed nine ways to Sunday and pregnant in no time," she laughs.

"That is correct," I agree. "But I will honor your wishes, my heart."

"All of them?" she asks, angling her face at me.

I grin down at her. "What is it you wish for, my Ni-Kee?"

"If I'm going to stay here—"

"If?" I growl the word, tightening my grip on the muscled curve of her ass.

"I want to be a warlord, too. I want the equivalent of my rank on Earth here. I can't just sit around and do nothing. I want to do what I was trained to do."

"You would undergo the trials to become a warlord?"

"Do women not do that?" Her tone is accusatory, and I blink in surprise.

"Of course they do. But a human has not."

"I can do it."

I nod once, thinking it over. "If that is what you wish, then so be it, my heart." I scrape my teeth over the tender spot under her jaw, savoring her soft moan.

"It is."

I lift her easily, and she wraps her legs around my bare torso, her heat seeping into my skin.

"I thought you wanted a bath," I say, amused and aroused. The tip of my cock prods against her, and she leans forward, biting my neck. I groan, the sensation of her blunt teeth nipping at my skin heating my blood.

"I do. But I wanted a hug, too."

"This is not a normal embrace," I inform her. "But if you like, I can think of another embrace I would accept from you?"

"Oh?" she pants, her legs tightening around me, her muscles twitching. "What's that?"

"I want to sink into your wet heat and feel you clench all around me with my name on your lips."

Her whole body shudders, and I smirk, my possessiveness roaring to life.

"I want to wipe away the memory of that bastard's hands on your skin, of his words in your ears. I want to replace them with me, filling you so deeply you can hardly breathe."

Instead of biting me again, or even grinding against me, Niki slumps, her head limp on my shoulder.

Worry tightens my shoulders, and I walk her into my circular bedroom. Morning light streams through the clear apertures, illuminating the dusting of brown spots across her nose and cheeks.

"I was so scared," she says, and wetness drips down my shoulder. "I thought you were hurt, or dead, and I couldn't stand the thought of it." Her chin tilts up at me, and my heart stutters with love.

"Ni-Kee," I murmur, pressing my lips against the droplet of eye water on her exposed cheek. "I was scared for you. I was proud of you and terrified all at once. The Roth… they will come for your people, once word gets out about your compatible biology."

"We can't let it happen to anyone. They are…"

"They are a troubled species," I finish the thought for her. "It would not be pleasant for the human females."

"Draz," she says, peppering my face with tiny kisses that send pinpricks of awareness through my body. "I love you. I love you so much, more than I ever thought possible."

"Be honest, my heart, you did not think it was possible to love me at all a week and a half ago."

She grins up at me, and I pick a leaf from her braid. "Oh, is that right?"

"Very right," I say solemnly. "And I am very glad that my courtship proved just how wrong you were."

"Your courtship?" she huffs, disentangling her legs from my body. "This is what you consider courtship?"

"I brought you can-dee. I fed you, kept you safe—"

At this, she holds up a hand. "One word. Snails."

"The snails were not a part of my courtship plan," I admit. "But I did nurse you back to health, and feed you many bowls of broth, and I helped you when you were too weak to walk to do your—"

"Draz!" she says, grinning and shaking her head. "Don't bring that up."

I clutch her tightly to me. "I will take care of you, my Ni-Kee. Forever. It will be my privilege and my honor."

She sighs, melting into me. A stick caught in her snarled hair jabs me in the throat, and I pluck it out, tossing it on the floor.

"Perhaps you should bathe now."

Laughing, she backs up, sniffing at her armpits. "I thought you like the way I smell. Actually, it seems like all you Suevans do, which, quite frankly, is weird as fuck."

"I do, and we do, and it is normal as fuck."

She laughs harder at this, her eyes creased as she smiles. The laughter dies, and she runs a hand through her tangles.

"I'm worried for my crew member that's still out there."

"I understand. Take care of your body, and I will arrange for food and clothes while you bathe, and then you can meet your crew and tackle the problem as you see fit."

My tail lashes back and forth. "And I will send word that you wish to undergo the trials and become the second warlord to Edrobaz. No one will dare cross a mated pair of warlords."

Her smile turns vicious, and I return it with pleasure before steering her to the door that leads to the bathing room.

Her eyes widen as she takes it in, a small sigh of happiness escaping her.

"I think I could get used to this," she says, and my heart fills with joy at the words.

CHAPTER
THIRTY-SIX

NIKI

EVERYTHING ABOUT EDROBAZ SURPRISES ME. The way the Suevans meld technology and nature is impressive and cohesive, the living trees that house them intimidating and beautiful. The 'bathing room,' as Draz called it, has running water, though I can't figure out how they manage to pump it all the way up here, nor how seamless everything is, wooden and stone and a glass-like substrate that lets both fresh air and light through while still acting like solid matter.

I bet Carmen's having a field day.

I towel off my hair, the cloth so unlike any fiber I've used before that if Draz hadn't pointed it out to me, I wouldn't have known that's what it was for. It's thin and stretchy, but manages to soak nearly all the excess water from me.

"Food is here, my heart," Draz calls, and my stomach rumbles at the mere mention of it. My limbs are limp and wobbly with exhaustion, and all I want to do is stuff my face and curl up in a ball next to Draz and sleep off the remnants of my snail given weakness.

I roll my shoulders back. It's out of the question. I need to eat and get dressed and find out who is missing from my crew as soon as possible, break the news that we can't return to Earth, and try to convince my crew that we can make the best of this world.

That I love Draz.

That I'm happier than I've ever been.

I swallow hard. It's not going to be an easy conversation, no matter how happy I am, because I know them. They'll like having their choices and future taken away as little as I did, and I've come out on top, married to an alien I've managed to fall head over heels for.

"Draz," I yell out, "can you bring me something to wear?"

He enters a moment later, something flimsy and teal in his hands. "I had this sent up, too. It's Suevan style, but you can order whatever you like when you return."

I take the garment from him, shaking it out.

It's a dress. A barely-there dress, so at odds with the sports bra and cargo pants that I've been stuck in for the last week and a half that I hardly know what to do with it.

"Here," he says, noticing my consternation and flashing a bit of fang in a smile. "I will help you."

His hands skate over my shoulders, the mounds of my breasts, his finger running along the inside of the thin towel until it drops away, baring my body to him.

Anticipation immediately fills me, and I clench my thighs against the arousal building there.

"Ni-Kee," he runs his thumbs over my nipples, and I let out a small gasp. "I cannot concentrate when your smell begs me to taste you."

"The dress," I manage, smooshing the diaphanous against my chest and pushing his wandering hands away. "Help me put it on. The sooner I can talk to my crew, the sooner you can have your way with me."

"Have my way with you?" he all but purrs, his diamond-pupils growing, his cock bulging against his pants. "I do like the sound of that."

His lips press against my forehead, and I lean into it, drawing comfort from him. I need all my strength for the conversation I'm about to have.

"Hold up your arms," he says, and I comply, raising an eyebrow as he drapes the fabric across my body.

"This doesn't cover very much," I say, plucking at the sheer blue fabric barely containing my breasts. I bite my lip, his talons trailing over the sides of my waists, the flare of my hips.

"It is not supposed to." His eyes are heated with desire, and moisture floods between my legs.

"Why not?" I say, my voice higher than usual. God, my crew is going to laugh their asses off when they see me in this. I run my hands over the front, trying to ignore the pulsing at the apex of my legs. Deliciously soft, the fabric is light and airy, and though I'm showing a lot of skin, all my important bits are covered.

"Because it is quite warm in the jungle. And because Suevans are proud of their bodies. As you should be, my perfect mate."

"We're on a mountain top. It's not nearly as hot up here."

"Ah, you think that because you have not been in the city. The atmospheric dome controls temperature and keeps it warmer for us, the way Suevans like it."

"Atmospheric dome?" I scrunch my nose and peer out the window, perplexed. "You mean to tell me there is an atmospheric dome over us right now?"

"Yes. Do you not use them on your Earth?"

I shake my head, snorting. "No. We wouldn't even know where to start with something like that."

"You like it here, yes, my heart?" His face is etched with worry, and I smooth a finger over his cheek.

"I do. You're here."

His hands trace lightly over my exposed back, and I shiver as tingles of pleasure race over my skin. How have I become so quickly addicted to him, to his touch? To the way he acts like I hung the moon?

I roll my shoulders back, bracing my hands along his wrists. "I have to go talk to my crew. Have you heard anything about how they are getting along?"

His mouth scrunches to the side, and he shakes his head. "No one knows we are here yet except the staff that brought the food and your dress. Will you at least take some food with us to eat?"

"Us? Are you going to show me where they are?"

His eyes narrow, a grin tugging up the side of his mouth. "Do you know where they are and how to navigate Edrobaz?"

"No," I admit, feeling stupid. "Of course not."

His chest puffs out with pride. "Then yes, I am coming. And I will carry food and feed you carefully, so that you can take in the sights as we walk without ruining your new dress."

"Draz, we're not going to have time to sight see."

His face falls. "I understand."

"Not until after I talk to them," I relent, poking his hard stomach. "Then you can show me around."

"Are you sure you are strong enough?"

"For a warlord, you sure are an overbearing grandmother."

"I am very confused about what humans must think an ancient woman with two generations of offspring do."

I snort, unable to stay serious about that translation fail. "I promise that if I get too tired, I'll let you carry me back here."

"So that I may have my way with you," he adds, a gleam in his eyes.

"Sure, yes," I say, grinning. "Sounds like a plan."

"It is a very good plan."

"Well then, let's get our food to-go and head out to my crew."

I pluck at the sheer skirts again, sliding into some overlarge leathery sandals Draz plopped on the floor for me, and trying to figure out how the hell I'm going to deal with the fallout.

It's time to be Captain Jacks again.

Only this edition is in love with an alien and wearing a barely-there gown.

Right.

CHAPTER
THIRTY-SEVEN

NIKI

BY THE TIME I get to the tree house, the myza, my crew is staying in, news of our arrival has spread. Suevans, mostly male, save for a handful of much older females, line the streets, watching our progress.

Draz nods to them, greeting them here and there with words of greeting or the strange fist thumps that the Suevans do out of respect.

Many of the Suevans openly stare at me, curiosity clear in their gazes.

It makes me worried about what, exactly, my crew has been up to, if humans are still such a rarity here that I'm gawked at. Have they stayed inside the whole time? Are they allowed out and about?

What the hell has been going on while I was stuck recuperating in the Suevan jungle?

The skirts of the dress flutter around my legs with every step, slits up both sides showcasing a whole lot more skin than I realized when Draz helped me get into it back at his myza. Our tree house.

"Ready?"

I nod once, throwing my shoulders back and steeling myself.

Draz presses a seam on the outside of the house my team's been bedding down in, and a door swings open.

The six women who made it to Edrobaz lounge around the interior. Food stretches across a long table made from a halved log, and velvety, moss-covered couches dot the floor. Everyone stops as I enter the room, and we're silent as we regard each other. I count the faces in front of me, trying to figure out who's missing.

"Oh thank God," Bex screams. "Captain Jacks is here, and she's dressed like a total skank!"

Okay, then.

Relief floods me. My crew seems healthy. About half of them are wearing dresses like mine, though a couple wear flowing pants and crop tops. Bex has a jagged wound down her side, and I move toward her instinctively.

"What happened?"

"Dergoz happened," she says acidly.

"Dergoz?" I glance back at where Draz is attempting to melt into the brown walls.

"The brute. The warlord I'm apparently married to." Bex peers around me, narrowing her eyes at Draz. "How's married life treating you?"

"Draz, can you give us some privacy?" I ask, and he nods once before slipping out of the house.

All the women in front of me give a silent sigh of relief, and I soak them in. Their faces are upturned to me like flowers seeking sun, and I'm so fucking glad to see them all that I just take a minute, scanning each of them.

"Has anyone else been hurt by the Suevans?"

Six heads shake, and I narrow my eyes at Bex.

"Didn't you just say that Dreg—" I stumble over the name.

"Dergoz didn't mean to. They call him a brute, but he's not one," she says quickly, and Michelle, our analyst, rolls her eyes.

"How fucked are we, Captain Jacks?" Michelle asks quietly, and as soon as I meet her eyes, her tired, angry eyes, I know she's already figured out the answer to that question and has likely been waiting for me to deliver the news.

"You look like shit," Bex adds unhelpfully.

"I had an encounter with a toxic alien species. And as far as I see it, we're only as fucked as we want to be." I wince. That didn't come out right.

A few chuckles and sidelong glances go around the room.

"Here's how I see it, and how I bet Michelle has already figured, too. Earth sold us out."

No murmurs, no shock, nothing.

"The Suevans are dying out. Some kind of virus mutated their genes, and females stopped being born. They reached out to Earth, and Earth promised to send compatible humans in exchange for their tech, which, after being here, I can agree we need desperately." I clear my throat. "The Suevans didn't know that we weren't informed about our purpose here."

"How do you know that?"

"Have none of you talked to your—" I pause. "Your Suevan?"

"You mean our accidental husbands? Our arranged marriage spouses?" Bex provides sweetly. I glare at her, and she winks at me.

"We can't talk to them," Michelle says. "Our translators failed."

I open my mouth. Close it again. "What?"

"Our translators didn't take," Tati, our medic, repeats. "The tech failed. Have you been able to talk to them?"

"Fucking hell," I mutter, running my hand through my hair and pacing. "Yes, I've been able to talk to them." No wonder my crew's holed up here, and the Suevans I saw this morning look at me like the circus came to town.

Fuck.

"They've been communicating with us through binary,"

Carmen says, patting the curly pouf on top of her head. She's wearing a pretty coral top and pant set that looks gorgeous against her skin. "It takes a long ass time for us to translate it, though."

"They're trying to find us tech that will work or update the receivers we already have." Tati's nimble fingers dance across her long, glossy black hair as she braids it off her face. "But as far as the wedding shit goes, we haven't bothered asking about any of it. What's the point? They think we belong to them."

"Did your… Are you sure none of you were hurt? At all?" I ask again, putting on my no nonsense face.

Despite the seriousness of my question, Bex snorts. "I'm sorry. But that expression and that outfit do not match."

"It's not funny, Bex," one of my crew pipes up, and several nod in agreement. "Just because you tried to fuck your alien doesn't mean the rest of us want to."

Bex's smile disappears, and she crosses her arms over her chest.

"When can we get back to Earth?" someone calls out.

Michelle meets my eyes, her expression grim.

Yep. She already figured it out.

"We can't get back to Earth."

Conversation explodes, angry words and shouts slamming against my ears. I wait for it to die down, to explain.

"They'll kill us," Michelle says softly, and half the room shuts up.

"What?" one of the crew in the back says, glaring at Michelle. "What did she say?"

"She said they'll kill us," I tell her. "And she's right. Think about it. They sold us out. It's fucked up, but that's what they did. Earth is desperate for the tech, and…" I grit my teeth, exhaling as I decide to tell them everything. Michelle's eyes grow even more alarmed. "And they should be. Earth is going to be enslaved or worse if they don't get it. And even if they do get the tech they need, we can't just show back up."

"Why not?" It's my surly mechanic talking, her hands on her hips and her face a rictus of frustration.

"Because no one can find out the truth of what the Federation did, selling us to Sueva. If we go back and they think for one minute we'll talk, they will kill us. That's what will happen. As soon as we got into Suevan space and took part in that ceremony, we became persona non grata to the Federation. So unless you want them to take us all out as collateral damage, we can't go back."

Stunned silence greets this, and the mechanic buries her face in her hands, another crew member drawing her into her chest to comfort her.

Tati's face is drawn, and Bex looks murderous.

I glance around for Gen, waiting to hear her rant and rave.

Shit.

"Gen's the one who didn't make it back," I say softly.

Michelle nods, and Carmen pinches the bridge of her nose.

Fucking hell. My best friend, lost in that jungle, with Crigomar rampaging through it, with a bad attitude and an unwanted Suevan husband.

It's less than ideal.

"We were taking bets on whether or not she's killed her husband by now. We did for you, too, but it seems like…" Bex trails off, clearly at a loss for what to say next.

I heave a sigh. "The Suevans are good people."

"They're fucking lizard people!" someone shouts, and a few of my crew laugh.

"Draz saved my life," I tell them. "I fell in love with him, and he loves me. I am honoring the mating ritual, and I'm going to become a warlord of Edrobaz."

Bex's eyebrows lift so high I wonder if they'll take flight. No one says anything, but Michelle purses her lips speculatively.

"What's the sex like?" Bex asks, a manic gleam in her eyes.

Some of the tension dissipates at the question, though

Carmen looks near tears. Tati's hands are clenched so tight her knuckles are white.

"Listen, team, I am not going to force any of you to remain married. No one will. Draz was disgusted and furious when he realized we hadn't volunteered for this mission, that we didn't even know what we were here for. But these are good, honest people, and they won't force you to do... anything you don't want to."

Bex nods, like she's all too well aware of it. "And now you can translate for us," she adds.

"I'm working on a solution for that, too," Carmen says. "Tati and I both are. There's no real reason why they shouldn't work, according to the tech scans we've made, so we're just going to keep at it."

"Okay, that's good." My chest heaves. "I can't begin to tell you how relieved I am that you all made it safe to Edrobaz. But there's another problem." My lips are dry, and I lick them, wishing Draz was here to help me explain this.

"Jesus fucking Christ," Bex says, raising an eyebrow. "It's worse than being sold off to Suevans for tech?"

"The Roth know we're compatible with them, too. With their species." Yeah, nothing like ripping off the Band-Aid.

"Oh, fuck," Michelle says, rubbing her eyes. "Fuck, fuck, fuck."

"Don't say that in front of any Suevans once you have your translators working," I tell her. "Or better yet, just don't say it at all." I nod my head.

Bex eyes take on a mischievous gleam.

"How do the Roth know that?" Carmen asks, and her lashes bat like she's fighting back tears.

"Because there was one here. After us."

"Earth has to get that tech," Michelle says.

Nods of agreement meet her assessment.

"It's already on the way, according to Draz." I resist wringing my hands in worry. All it would take is one well-placed Roth ship to kill any hope for Earth.

"If it doesn't get blown up." Michelle's mouth twists to the side, like when she's presented with a particularly tangled problem. "We need these translators to work."

"I agree," I tell her. "Getting your translators working is top priority." I raise my voice making sure everyone can hear me. "Making sure we can communicate with Earth is the next priority. Carmen, Tati, and Bex, you three are my science officers. You'll need to partner with the Suevans to ensure we can get plans to Earth to engineer their own defense system should the Suevan transport be shot down by Roth ships."

I take a deep breath, and everyone's eyes are on me, purpose in their eyes, in the way they stand.

Good.

"We might not have signed up for all the elements of this mission, but we still have our original mission to carry out. We need to work with the Suevans, and we need to ensure Earth has everything they need before the Roth get there."

"Aye-aye Captain," they group says as one.

I nod at them, dismissing them from the impromptu meeting.

"Are you going to be staying with us?" Bex asks, coming to stand in front of me. "Or with your alien?"

"His name is Draz, and I'll be staying with him." My stomach tightens with delicious anticipation.

"What's it like? Is it like that book I shared with you?" Her eyebrows wiggle mischievously, and for a second, I wonder what exactly went down between her and her alien husband.

"Er," I say, trying to figure out what to say.

"Did he touch you with his tail?" she whispers, grinning.

Deep crimson blush heats my chest and cheeks, and I bite my lip at the memory.

"I knew it!" Her fist pumps through the air. "Lucky."

"Bex," I say, exasperated.

"Sorry, that was inappropriate, huh? Insubordinate?" She laughs.

"I think we're past insubordination at this point." My voice softens. "It was good. He's a good man."

Bex clasps her hands to her chest. "Sounds kinky. And romantic." A wistful sigh tears out of her. "Say, you wouldn't mind translating for me and Dergoz, would you?"

"I wouldn't, but I'm not sure either of us are going to have much time to do that."

"Right. Right, of course not. I'll work with Tati and Carmen on the translator issue. And the other aliens, too." She shrugs offhandedly, her easy acceptance only sparking my curiosity more.

I take a deep breath and let some of my officer façade slip. "So there's been no word of Gen? None at all?"

Bex's face turns grim, and she gnaws her lower lip, her hands on her hips. "No. Nothing. Though it was the same for you, and then you show up here, safe and sound." She shrugs. "Well, other than your run-in with toxic snails… is that what you said? Please tell me you didn't eat a snail."

I make a choking sound, the mere thought of chomping on one of those things making my stomach turn. "No. I didn't try to eat one."

"Phew. There's hope for you yet, Captain Jacks." She winks up at me, then frowns again. "You're worried about Gen?"

"She's tough," I say, unwilling to voice the fact that yes, I am very concerned about my best friend and first officer.

"She is. And you know what? She has a Suevan with her. She'll be okay. I bet he's super invested in keeping her alive, right?" She wiggles her eyebrows a little, but it lacks her normal verve. Her arms cross, and she hugs them to herself.

"You all right?" I ask, tilting my head.

"Yeah," she says brightly. "Why wouldn't I be? I have an unwilling alien husband and a whole new planet, and if I ever return home, I'll be murdered. What's not to be happy about?"

Right.

"Unwilling?" I squint at her.

"You know what I mean," she says, making a shooing gesture with her hand.

I really, really don't, but I can tell Bex isn't about to say anything else on the subject.

"What about you?" she asks, furrowing her brow. "Are you okay?"

I shouldn't answer honestly, not as her commanding officer. But we're not Federation anymore, not really, and it might just give her some hope.

"I am," I say. "I really am. I'm worried about Gen and you all, and the Roth, of course, but I'm good. Really good."

"Good," she says, sounding abnormally listless. "That's good."

"Gen's probably bossing around her Suevan and being her usual hardcore self. Even a prince won't be able to handle her." I say, and smile to myself.

"Wait, wait, wait." Bex holds up a hand, and Michelle sidles closer, her eyes wide. "Did you say prince? Gen is married to a Suevan prince." She snorts, covering her face with her hands. "What the fuck?" she yells, the sound muffled by her palms.

"Oh. Yeah." I shoot Michelle a look, my eyebrows furrowed in consternation.

Michelle sighs and jerks her head, indicating we should move away from Bex.

"What happened?" I ask her, glancing back at Bex, who's muttering to herself and wandering off to the table full of food.

"She was into her alien." Michelle's nostrils flare. "I think she thought it was going to be like one of her books… you know the ones."

I nod, trying to act like it wasn't like that for me, not at all. "Uh-huh."

"I think she's just disappointed that it didn't turn out like that for her. Add Gen marrying an alien prince, and it's probably too much."

"Honestly, there doesn't seem to be that big of a difference between the prince and the warlords."

"What do you mean?" Michelle says, and Bex creeps back over, her eyes wide.

"The warlords... we all married warlords, except for Bex."

"Warlords," Michelle echoes. "And they all live...here. In this city?"

Trust my intel specialist to point out a problem I hadn't even thought of. My throat bobs as I swallow, and her eyes narrow.

"No... This is Draz's territory." And mine, I almost say, but I don't want to, er, alienate them.

"What's going to happen when they need to leave to go back to their territories?" Michelle asks, her eyes calculating.

I blow out a breath. "We can cross that bridge when we come to it," I say. "For now, let's focus on communication and getting that tech to the Federation. No one is leaving here until we're sure we can keep Earth out of Roth control. Yes?"

"Yes ma'am," Michelle says, all those years of Federation training pulling the response from her instantly.

"What if we want to leave?" Bex asks, and I swing my gaze to her. "I mean, are you even our CO now? What's the chain of command?"

"She's our Captain," Michelle snaps. "That's the chain of command. We came here for a mission, and that mission isn't complete."

"Aye-aye," Bex says limply.

I raise one eyebrow, and she snaps off a salute.

"I'll talk to Draz about what happens if you want to leave with your warlords," I relent. Uneasy, I turn the idea over in my head. Draz reassured me that he, at least, wouldn't force the issue of our arranged marriage. But what if he's the only one who feels that way—what if a Suevan forces the issue and takes one of my crew?

Bex is waiting for an answer, her eyes narrowing.

"Do you have reason to believe one of the Suevans is planning to take one of us?"

Michelle shrugs one shoulder. "Nothing concrete."

Fuck. I don't like the sound of that. "Which one?"

"It's more than one."

I run a hand through my hair. It's drying in loose waves around my shoulders, and I'm so unused to it being down that it throws me for a momentary loop.

"Will it set off an internal conflict if you and your warlord don't allow the other Suevans to take us?" Michelle asks, her fingers pulling at the gauzy fabric of her loose pants.

"We didn't have a lot of time to discuss alien politics or what happens next. I was too concerned with making sure you were all physically safe and dealing with the Roth kidnapping."

"Don't forget your poison snails." Michelle's tone is light, but her lips are pressed thin, belying her worry.

"Yeah," I cringe, my hands fingering the rough patch of still-healing skin. "That, too. Let's take it one day at a time."

Michelle blinks, and I know her ridiculously overpowered brain is sorting through a million possible scenarios. "I'll try to dig up anything I can on politics and precedent."

How she's planning to do that without a working translator, I don't have a clue, but if anyone can do it, it's Michelle.

Bex nods, unhappy but not mutinous.

Thank God.

I do not want to deal with mutiny. I need them focused and working towards protecting Earth.

Even if Earth and the Federation did fuck us over. And in Gen's case, fucked us over royally.

CHAPTER
THIRTY-EIGHT

DRAZ

THE UNDERGROUND PRISON'S cooler than the rest of Edrobaz, designed to be uncomfortable for any Suevans who find themselves on the wrong side of our laws. Not torturous, but a constant, nagging coldness that nips at my scaled hide.

Blue lights bounce through the clear flexiglass cell, an impenetrable membrane that allows sound and light to pass, but not, say, an angry Roth. The cool temperature likely will not bother him the same way it would a Suevan, but he is anything but comfortable.

The Roth is furious. He doesn't speak, but his grey nostrils flare slightly as I stand in front of his cell. His chest is bandaged, and black blood seeps through the wound my mate so efficiently placed.

Dergoz stirs next to me. Always ready to fight, Dergoz exudes a feral energy that's fully honed on the prisoner in front of us. We called him the Brute in our wars against Roth on the settled planets, a title he fully earned, willing to do anything against the Roth to seize the advantage.

I thought he was over the top then, but he's even more on edge now.

Likely from the frustration of not being able to mate his female. Guilt slides through me, oily and slick. Finding out that my Ni-Kee is the only one able to understand our language still, through some fluke of the implant programming, has left me both counting my lucky stars and saddened for my fellow Suevans.

A door closes softly, and footsteps sound against the stone floors.

"Has he spoken yet?" Alvez asks. He turns towards the cell, the blue lights illuminating a criss-cross of scars along his scaled back. The Suevan spent time in the Roth fighting pits, taken as a child on a settlement and raised as a gladiator slave. The male has every reason to wish the Roth a brutal death, and yet, he appears the most in control of us all.

"No."

"And he was working with the southern Suevans?"

Dergoz makes a rasping noise of disbelief, clicking his talons along his crossed arms. "I cannot believe they would be so foolish as to believe anything that came from that poisoned tongue."

"The Roth have long been persuasive," Alvez answers, his eyes full of cold, calculating rage. "I am sure he made his promises seem as sweet as they were false."

"He threatened to take my mate," I say, and both males turn to look at me. "He did not know the human females were compatible, or if he did, he made a show of not knowing it, and offering her a place as a bed slave and breeder with him." My knuckles crack as I tighten my fists at the memory.

Alvez's hand clasps my shoulder, offering strength and solidarity. "He did not succeed."

"I worry, my friend," I tell him, my heart speeding up and my tail smacking against the floor. "I worry that the Roth know, and that they head for our women, even now. Or Earth, to harvest as many females as they can and once again become a mighty foe."

"Our transport to Earth—you think they tail it, even now?"

"It is a possibility," I admit.

"We need those females," Dergoz growls. "Our males need mates."

"What are you suggesting?" Alvez says, his eyebrows drawing up.

"If the human males cannot protect their women, then they do not deserve them." Dergoz the Brute's tail slams into the rock floor, sending vibrations through the facility and setting the lights to flickering.

"That is not our choice to make." I narrow my eyes at the male, exasperated. "The females cannot be taken. We will not stoop to the level of the Roth. Not now, not ever."

Dergoz makes a fist, slamming it into his open hand. "The Roth are not the only ones whose numbers dwindle. We must reclaim our place in this galaxy, and the human females are the key. They are not treasured on Earth. Their people sent them here like troblek to slaughter, without a clue of what we intended for them."

Alvez makes a sound of agreement, and I cock an eyebrow at him. "You agree with this plan? To pillage Earth for females?"

"I agree that their Federation deceived them, and that our mates have been dealt out a great wrong. But I do not think *brute* force is the correct path to the females." He puts an extra emphasis on the word, and Dergoz growls, his muscles bunching in irritation.

"Then what is it you think best, gladiator?" Dergoz rasps, challenge inherent in the question.

By the Suevan skies, Having all the warlords together in Edrobaz is volatile. We're too used to command, to working independently of each other, since our time together in the settlements fighting off the Roth. Not to mention, these males are strung tightly, shedding frustration like so much skin during a youth's first molt.

Alvez steps closer to Dergoz, menace radiating through him. "This gladiator thinks that we should use our brains. The human females are clearly unused to being treasured. The ones we already have are our greatest lever for the rest of the human females. We lavish our mates with affection and gifts, and they will in turn spread the word back to Earth. Then we can begin offering places to select Earth women here, where we can pair them up with males of our own."

Dergoz grunts, a calculating expression in his gaze.

"This is not poorly conceived," I say. "But it does not solve the problem of the Roth."

Alvez faces the cell once more, and the Roth stares us down, his black hair flaring around his shoulders, buffeted by a nonexistent wind.

Damn energy manipulators.

"No, it does not," Alvez says. "We need to send a contingent of Suevans to guard the transport."

"I can send a team," Dergoz says, his tail slapping against the floor again.

I try not to sigh in annoyance. Dergoz is clearly angling to pair his warriors up with humans first.

Alvez snorts in amusement, one brow raised. He runs a finger across the straps of the weapons slung across his chest. "I can also send warriors."

"We send warriors from each clan," I say. "And we send a few southern Suevans, too."

"They are traitors," Dergoz's eyes light up with fury.

"They are Suevan, and we have done wrong by them if they thought to turn to the Roth instead of to us. We must mend this broken bridge between us if we hope to stand strong against the Roth's eventual assault."

"The prince will want to send some from his clan," Alvez says.

I nod my agreement. "We need to find him and his female."

"I will go," Dergoz says, and I tilt my chin, considering the male.

"You would leave your mate?"

"Aye."

"There are Crigomar out there. You would risk yourself and your future?"

Dergoz's expression grows thunderous. I stand my ground. "Until my mate can understand me, there is no point to putting her in harm's way."

Harm's way? Does he think himself a danger to her?

I shake my head. "It is your choice. If you want to search for Prince Kanuz and the female warrior Gen, then so be it."

"And the Roth?" Alvez asks.

"Find out what you can," I say curtly. "I know you are best equipped for dealing with their tricks." Years of enslavement to the Roth has left Alvez with deep scars, but there is no one with better insight into how the Roth's mind works, a point we made good use of during the settlement wars.

Alvez nods once, and I turn to leave, Dergoz lagging along in my wake.

I am ready to leave this business for the moment, to turn my mind to more pleasurable pursuits.

Like the surprise I have in store for my precious mate.

Like the pleasure I intend to wring from her supple body afterwards.

CHAPTER
THIRTY-NINE

NIKI

I BLINK into the hot Suevan sun, the humidity settling on my shoulders like a damp towel. Draz isn't waiting outside, like I thought he would be. Instead, an older Suevan waits for me, her white hair piled high on her head.

"You must be Ni-Kee," she says, smiling warmly at me.

"That's me," I say, pushing back the urge to correct her. Captain Jacks doesn't exist here, not the same way. There's no reason to insist she call me by that name, the title that the Federation threw in the garbage. "Where is Draz?"

"He stepped away to tend to some warlord business," the older woman tells me, a calculating glint in her eyes.

"Right." Annoyance slips under my skin. Why didn't he wait for me? He knows I want to lead here, too. Is there something he's keeping from me? It rankles.

"I'm Cephi," the Suevan says, still smiling. "Draz told me to take you into the market so that you can pick out new bedding and whatever other things you like to make his myza feel like home."

"Ah," I say.

My disappointment and irritation must show in my face, because Cephi laughs, her tail flicking behind her. "You humans are so expressive."

"Did he say why he isn't coming with me?" It's not her fault I'm annoyed with him, feeling lost and small that he hasn't included me in whatever he's doing today.

"He did not. He did seem in a hurry to get back to you, though, so I would not be surprised if he meets us at the market. Then I am sure you can ask him as many questions as you see fit regarding his whereabouts." The Suevan female gives me a knowing look, and I sigh.

I never in a million years thought I'd be what amounts to a kept woman, dressed in next to nothing and sent to shop while the menfolk make all the decisions.

It burns. I hook a finger in the material around my neck, tugging at it like it will help ease the sudden tightness in my throat.

"Come now, Ni-Kee, let us find some fine things. It is a beautiful day, and there is no sense in wasting it."

Cephi gestures for me to follow her, and I do, letting her chatter wash over me as she leads me through the mostly empty streets.

"Where is everyone?" I ask, and Cephi glances sidelong at me.

"He did not tell you of the troubles our people have faced?"

"Oh, he did. I just expected more Suevans. This city is large."

"Our numbers dwindle. Where there were once tens of thousands, now we are in the mere hundreds here." Her pain is visible, her voice seeped in it.

"I'm sorry," I say softly. "I didn't intend to upset you."

"It is not you I am upset with, Ni-Kee." She sighs, and we round a corner, where a bustling marketplace awaits. Though the street could likely hold hundreds more, it's still rather full of Suevans going about their business.

The smell of spiced meats mingles with the scent of hundreds of flowers, the colorful bolts of Suevan fabric competing with polished pieces of Suevan armor. One vendor hawks personal comms devices, and another displays delicate jewelry that doubles as weapons. Gen would love that.

My jaw drops, my eyes roaming the place, trying to take it all in.

Cephi prods my arm, and her eyes laugh when I meet her gaze.

"Well then, Ni-Kee, shall we find some new things for your new home?"

"I don't really know where to start."

"That's all right, I certainly do," the Suevan says briskly, setting off for a stand stacked high with bolts of fabric.

She speaks with enough authority that I follow her, curious about who, exactly, she is to my Draz.

"The human female is the warlord's mate," Cephi announces loudly, and dozens of Suevans pause, all turning to get a good look at me. "We need items to help make his myza worthy of her presence. Pillows, I think. New blankets. She will need gowns and pantsuits, too. Perhaps some cooking equipment—"

"Armor and weapons," I interrupt her. "I'm not a good cook."

"That's all right," Cephi says, looking at me with that sly amusement. "My son will be a good enough cook for both of you. We should bring him some new tools though, he will like that."

My eyebrows shoot up, and I swallow hard, feeling every inch the idiot.

"Why didn't you tell me you were his mother?" I wince, the words coming out too loud.

"I found it humorous to wait. I wanted to see what you were like, without any added pressure."

I narrow my eyes at her. "Did you find out anything interesting?"

"Just that my son has made a very good match, indeed." She

grins at me. "Welcome to Edrobaz, Ni-Kee. Go choose your weapons, if you wish. We can discuss garments and bedding once you've looked your fill at the sharper things."

I bite my cheeks, trying not to become irritated at her overbearing tone. Unfortunately, I'm running on little sleep, too much stress, and am annoyed beyond reason with the fact that Draz left me without a word, not even giving me a heads up that his mother would be waiting for me.

"We're already here, so I'll pick out a few things now. I need clothes just as much as I need weapons." The tone of command rings through the words, but Cephi's grin only grows.

"Good, very good," she says approvingly, and I belatedly realize it was a test to see if I'd back down to her or assert myself.

Good thing she *wanted* me to assert myself, because I am certainly *not* the type of woman to back down, human or otherwise.

I crack a grin at her, running my hands over a silky mint green material. "Did I pass your test?"

Her mouth twists to the side, her tail lashing behind her before she barks out a guttural laugh. "Yes, yes you did. Now then, let me show you how Suevans haggle. No one will make a fool of my long-awaited daughter, not while I draw breath. Isn't that right, Xez?"

We both look up at the vendor, who must be Xez. "Of course not, Cephi. No one will make a fool of the warlord's wife. Definitely not me." He shakes his head, offering me another bolt of even softer fabric, this one in a deep red. "I can make you a gown like the one you have on out of this. I have a few new designs that may be suited to your human form, too."

"Your clan has been the source of much gossip," Cephi tells me.

"My clan?" It takes my tired brain a minute to catch up. "Oh, my crew? Well, that doesn't surprise me. Have they come to the market then?"

"Not yet," Xez says, pulling out more fabric swatches in a rainbow of gorgeous colors. "But I long to dress them. Will you tell them that Xez has many ideas to clothe their bodies in?"

I blink at his odd word choice.

"Don't promise him anything," Cephi tells me, glaring at Xez. "He knows good and well that the human women can choose who clothes their bodies themselves."

"Of course they can," Xez retorts, diamond pupils narrowing in anger. "I simply wanted the First Warlord's wife to put in a good word. Is that not why you are here, Cephi? Because I am the best?"

Cephi makes a disgruntled noise, and I grin a little.

"I'll take three gowns and four pant and top outfits," I say. "In any of the colors you think will be best."

"You don't want to pick?" Xez sounds dismayed. "What if you don't like them?"

"She needs fifteen gowns and twenty pant sets," my mother-in-law says. "Give her one of each color."

I cut my eyes to her, trying to decide if this is another test, but she smiles down at me without any guile in her eyes.

"My son has gone too long without a mate. He will want you dressed in the best, and you need clothes, do you not, Ni-Kee? You will have many functions to attend."

"All right," I say slowly.

"Put it on my son's account," Cephi says. "Do not even think of marking it up."

Xez and Cephi begin haggling, and I wander over to the booth full of Suevan armor. I've only ever seen Draz wearing pants, and the thought of him in full armor makes my mouth go dry. My warlord is large and formidable enough without the armor, his scaled hide providing nearly all the protection he can need.

"Is it sold as a set?" I ask the vendor, slightly confused about why they have armor at all.

"We would have to create something special just for you," the vendor tells me. "No disrespect, human female, but our armor will not fit you."

I hadn't even considered armor for myself, but… now that he mentions it, that sounds perfect.

"Could you do it?" If the Roth show up, I know only too well how fragile my body is. I need to train with it on. My whole team does. I don't know how much money I have to spend today, but I'll need to discuss a budget for me and my team. None of us need to be bored.

Leaving Michelle and Bex bored is a recipe for disaster.

And really, we can't take much more of those.

My gaze flicks back to the vendor, who's measuring me up.

"Do you doubt my ability?"

"No, just your willingness." It's matter of fact, and the Suevan blinks in surprise.

"You are the warlord's mate. If you want the armor, you will have the armor. In fact, it will be an interesting diversion to create it for you. The first set will be free."

"That's not necessary."

"It is necessary. You may not like the way it moves. I know nothing of human bodies other than what my eyes are telling me."

"I'm not going to ask you to work for free," I argue back. Is this what Cephi meant when she said she would handle the negotiations?

"You aren't asking me to work for free, I am telling you I will be working for free."

"Accept the armor," Cephi says, her hand on my shoulder, her tone brooking no argument.

"I accept the armor," I say, unsure of what the hell has the vendor so riled up. "But let me buy a few things for Draz."

I select a shoulder piece, along with a pair of new pants, like the ones that are all but ruined after our trek through the jungle. Cephi haggles with him, bringing the price down to something that satisfies them both, then grins at me when the vendor sighs wearily and hands us a bag stuffed full.

"And that, Ni-Kee, is how it is done." She wipes her palms against each other, the gesture so human that I can't help grinning right back at her.

"What else do you want?" she says, a gleam in her eyes, like she's just getting warmed up for shopping.

"A nap," I say honestly, exhaustion wearing at me.

"You are not having a good time?" she asks, worry clear on her face. "Was I offensive?"

"No, no, not at all. We hiked all night, though, and I'm completely drained."

"Drained does not sound good. We can get you some refreshments?"

I crack a small grin at her misunderstanding. "I could do with something to drink, but I really just need sleep."

"Then we will get you a drink and take you right back to your myza." She nods at her words, tugging me along as Suevans stop and stare at the sight of us. Me, really, the lone human out and about.

I tug my dress further over my chest, suddenly self-conscious of all the skin I'm showing.

"What are you lot staring at?" Cephi snaps out, waving her hand. "Move along. This human's mated already."

There are a few grumbles and a few amused looks, but the flow of Suevans continues around us, and Cephi harrumphs, tugging me along to a stand at the end of the lane. Flower garlands hang heavy across the front of his cart, and my mouth waters at the fragrant smell.

"Two," Cephi orders, and within seconds, we each have a massive drink in our hands.

It looks so much like a fancy tropical drink I once ordered on a much-needed vacation that a blast of homesickness nearly stuns me. The exterior is reminiscent of a coconut shell, but larger and bright turquoise. A few pink petals bob in the icy slurry, and Cephi watches me from over her own drink.

"It is good, Ni-Kee. You will like it."

"Thank you," I tell her. "It was very kind of you to come with me and help introduce me to Edrobaz."

"What else would I do?" She shrugs, affronted. "You are my daughter now. We will shop together as often as you like. And I will spoil the children you give my son relentlessly, as is traditional."

I snort, then take a deep swig of the drink to avoid saying anything else. Anything like, *I don't know if I want kids*, because let's face it; I am not ready to have that conversation with my surprise of a mother-in-law.

The icy drink explodes across my tongue, sweet and tangy, somewhere between a lime and a watermelon. It's really good, and I drink deeply, enjoying it after days of only stale, sulfurous water.

"You like this?" Cephi asks, squinting down at me.

"Definitely."

"Good. Now let's take you back to the myza so you may regain your strength and begin making me grandbabies."

I better pace myself on the drink. If she keeps bringing up babies, I'm going to have to do something to keep my mouth busy or I'm going to get myself in trouble.

Cephi continues to talk, telling me the history of Edrobaz as I follow her through the city. I half-listen, thinking about what she said about babies.

What would it be like to have babies here? On an alien planet, with an alien warlord who ruthlessly stole my heart?

Would they have green, scaly skin like him, or my own soft human skin? Tails?

By the time we make it back to Draz's myza, my feet are aching, and I'm swaying with exhaustion. Sweat beads along my neck and the small of my back. Thank goodness the dress breathes. It would be unbearably hot in my normal uniform.

I stand at the door, nearly half-dead with the need to sleep, and Cephi opens it easily, then tugs me into a gentle hug.

"It makes an old female like me very happy to finally have a daughter," she tells me, pulling back to hold me at arms' length, inspecting my face. Her eyes shine with honesty and emotion, and I'm suddenly overwhelmed with a surge of gratitude.

"Thank you," I tell her, and her eyes widen with surprise as I tug her into another hug. "I didn't expect to have another mother, but I'm glad I've found one."

"Tchah, that's enough of that," she says, but looks pleased. She pushes me through the door. "Now get some sleep."

I do as she says, hustling through the bedroom door. The zoleh squeals as she sees me, pouncing and curling up on my chest. I run my fingers through her soft fur, and I pass out as soon as my eyes close.

CHAPTER
FORTY

DRAZ

THE MYZA IS quiet and dark when I get home, a cool respite after the scorching heat of the afternoon sun throughout the streets of Edrobaz. Packages pile high beside the door, proof that Ni-Kee and my mother had a fruitful day of shopping.

It gladdens my heart, to think of the two of them haggling with vendors and laughing as they took the upper hand in negotiations. I can only imagine that the two of them made a fearsome pair in the marketplace.

I cannot wait to see my mate. I've only been away from her a few short hours, but her absence chafes. Will I never have enough of her?

I think not.

The door to the mating room sways under my hand, opening easily. The last of the sunshine filters through the round openings, casting beams of light onto the bed.

Ni-Kee sleeps in the same clothes she left the house in this morning. Her hair spreads across the pillows, one arm flopped over her eyes as though she couldn't even be bothered to get comfortable before falling asleep. The zoleh's curled up in her hair, and neither stir as I walk into the room.

My poor, sweet mate. A smile curves my lips.

The rise and fall of her chest is slow and even, her mouth slightly parted.

I cannot resist this human female. Her skin begs to be touched, the pert peaks of her nipples asking for my mouth on them. I am obsessed with the taste of her, the luscious honey of her arousal.

Resisting the urge to run my fingers over that smooth skin, I quietly walk into the bathing room instead. Cool water pours overhead, and I take my time, sudsing my long hair and thinking on the day.

"Hi." Ni-Kee's voice startles me from my reverie, and I look up to find her smiling at me, her face still soft with sleep.

"My love," I say, affection and arousal riding me hard. The luxurious fabric of the dress clings to her erotic human curves, enhancing her already perfect body.

"Why did you leave me?" Her voice isn't accusatory, not quite, but there's an edge to it. "I thought you were going to wait for me, and then your mother was outside instead."

"You told me you wanted to spend time alone with your human females. I also had business to attend to." I shrug, confused. "Are you upset with me?"

She sighs, running her hands through her hair. "No, not upset. I just... Can you tell me what you plan to do next time? I just think we need to do better communicating. I didn't even know you had a mother."

"Where else would I have come from?"

"I don't know." She throws her hands in the air, clearly annoyed. "An egg?"

"An egg?" I choke out a laugh, water streaming into my eyes. A thought occurs to me, and I bite off my laugh. "Are humans born from eggs?"

"What? No! Why would we be born from eggs?"

"Why else would you think Suevans come from eggs?"

"Because you have scales!" She pinches the bridge of her nose. "No. This wasn't even about hatching—"

"We do not hatch. Is that what humans call birth? How curious." I turn the thought over in my head. Perhaps the scientists were wrong about the compatibility of our species. Not that I care, not for myself, anyway. Ni-Kee is mine.

"No, we don't call it hatching. Ugh! All I am trying to say is that I was surprised that you were gone, and then I didn't even know Cephi was your mother until she let it slip. The whole thing made me feel a little uncomfortable and like I was being tested. And I don't want that."

"My mother was unkind to you?"

"No, no, she was fine. It was just a surprise." She's waving a hand around, agitated.

I can resist her no longer. I snatch her wrist from the air, tugging her under the water with me. Ni-Kee lets out a delightful squeal, and I chuckle into her hair.

"I am sorry that you did not like my surprise. I was only trying to take care of things while you did. I thought you would like to meet my mother." I press a long kiss to her temple.

"I understand, I do."

"Next time, I will tell you, yes? And you will tell me what you plan, as well."

"Okay," she says, smiling up at me. Water beads on her nose and eyelashes, and I kiss them, too.

"My dress is getting all wet," she says.

"That is what happens when you stand under water," I tell her. My hands grip her waist, and I move them slowly up her sides. The water makes the already thin fabric cling to her curves, her nipples tight on the heavy curve of her breasts. I run the pads of my thumbs over them.

She shudders against my touch, letting out a low moan that my body immediately responds to.

"Are you wet here?" I ask her, palming her breasts until she makes the same delicious noise.

"Yes," she murmurs, her eyes heating.

"We should take this dress off then, yes?" I pull the cleverly tied strap from around her waist, then tug it forward, revealing her breasts.

A feral growl rips from my throat, and I can contain myself no longer. The rest of the dress falls away with one slash of my talons.

Ni-Kee's breath catches, and the addictive fragrance of her arousal fills the air.

"I cannot get enough of you," I tell her. "I am addicted to you. Obsessed. I crave you."

I drop to my knees, splashing in the thin layer of water. Nudging her knees apart with my own, I grip the curve of her ass, and she groans, leaning against the wall for support.

It's not enough.

I pull one leg over my shoulder, and then the other. Her hands curl in my hair. Her sex is fully exposed to me, glistening, glorious. I inhale, reveling in her.

"Are you wet here?" I ask, and she quivers on top of my shoulders.

"Yes," she says, her heels digging into my back as she arches up.

"So greedy." A throaty chuckle fans across her sex, and then I can hold back no longer.

My tongue meets her swollen, wet sex, the flavor bursting across my tongue better than anything else has ever tasted.

Ni-Kee cries out, clutching my hair, and her wild excitement sends a shiver through me.

I lick again, flicking the small nub of her pleasure with my tongue until she's moving her hips in time with it, her breathing ragged.

"Please, please, Draz," she whines.

But I do not let her come. Instead, I unhook her legs, sliding her down my body. She gasps, squirming against me. I suck one pink nipple into my mouth, biting just hard enough to elicit a needy groan.

"Please," she repeats.

"What is it you want, my mate?" I want to hear her say it. I want her to tell me she needs my cock as badly as I crave her cunt.

"You, Draz, I want you inside me. Please."

I smile at her, and then, with brutal efficiency, I line my cock up to her entrance and thrust deep.

"Yes, Draz, yes." Her fingernails scrabble against my shoulders, her sex clenching and fluttering all around me. My xof begins to vibrate, and she cries out, her noises increasingly wild.

"More," she says.

"More," I agree, nipping at her ear. I back away from the wall. Gripping her hips, I raise her up, then impale her on the hard shaft of my cock. Her cunt makes delicious, wet noises, and I growl my approval, thrusting harder, faster, as her body shakes and trembles with the nearness of release.

"Mine," I tell her. "You are mine forever, my Ni-Kee."

She shatters at that, sobbing my name, her entire body shaking from the force of her orgasm. "Yours," she says.

I savagely claim her mouth, still pounding into her, on the edge of release. I press my forehead to hers, staring in her eyes as I pull out and fall over the edge, my hot seed painting her breasts and stomach in white.

"I love you," she says. "And you're mine, too."

"I do not know what I did right to become yours, my sweet human, but I would do it again a thousand times, for a thousand years, for just one minute of your company."

I close my eyes, thanking the Suevan skies that my mate made her way onto my world.

CHAPTER
FORTY-ONE

NIKI

"SO, HOW WAS YOUR DAY?" I ask, then laugh at the relative normalcy of that question. I never thought I'd be asking my husband that, much less my alien husband. The alien stares at me, perplexed at my laughter.

"All my days are perfect now that you are in them." He pulls on the new pants I bought, running his palms down his thighs in appreciation. "These are nice."

"I am glad you like them, since your money paid for them."

"What's mine is yours, Ni-Kee."

"I know." And I do, but… "It feels weird to me. To be sent off shopping, to not work. I want to be your partner. Not just… your woman, you know?"

"You want to be a warlord, yes? I spoke to the Edrobaz elders, and they all agreed to your trial." He says it like it's no big deal, even shrugging one massive shoulder.

"You already set it up?" My jaw drops open, and I stop wrangling the new clothing to stare at him.

"What did you think I was doing today?" He takes the top from my hands, helping me put my arms through it, wrapping it around my body. "There. Now your breasts will stop distracting me."

"I thought maybe you went to interrogate the Roth." My hands rest on his forearms, and I stare up into his eyes.

Draz shifts guiltily, and I brush his hair off one shoulder. "I did that, too," he finally says.

"Why didn't you wait for me? I would have gone with you. What he says matters to me and my people, too." It stings, and I swallow it down, waiting. Draz has proven worthy of my trust.

"You're right," he says easily. "I thought time would be of the essence, however, and you were busy with your crew. You are welcome to come next time, if we try again. The Roth failed to offer up any information. We're sending a contingent of warriors to protect the tech transport all the way to Earth."

"Oh, wow," I say, my eyes widening. "Do you have the people to spare?"

He runs a thumb across my cheekbone, the touch so tender that I smile at him, regardless of the seriousness of the situation. "It is not about sparing my people, but about protecting the future of both of ours."

I lean into his touch, my eyes half closing. "My crew's translators don't work."

"I heard."

"We need to fix them." I open my eyes fully, pinning him with a hard stare. "And we need to talk about whether or not the other warlords plan to take them from here."

"What? What do you mean?" He looks truly dumbfounded at the notion. "Do your crew wish to leave with them? I was under the impression that no other couples had bonded."

"No, not as far as anyone said."

"Then why would you even ask—" He stops, staring at me with incredulity. "Your females will be easy to convince to come to Sueva, if this is how human males treat them."

"Is that part of the plan?" I laugh, sure he's joking. His

eyebrows raise, and my laugh dies. "You want to convince more women to come here?"

"I want *you* to convince them."

"Draz," I say, about to refuse... but then I think about it. Really think about it. If I'd come here to start a new life, not been tricked here with a lie, with the possibility of marrying a Suevan warrior, maybe I would have been more open to all of this? Who's to say women on Earth would be opposed to it?

"Tell me what you're thinking."

"I'm thinking that I would want to discuss it with my crew."

He waits, tilting his head.

"It doesn't sound like the most terrible idea in the whole world."

"High praise," he says seriously, then grins at me, wrapping his hands tight around my exposed midriff.

I lean against him, sighing at the familiar, welcome hard warmth of his chest. He's my home now.

"Tell me it's going to be okay," I say, knowing it's a stupid thing to ask. "Tell me the Roth aren't going to win."

"They have already lost," he says into my hair. "We have each other, and we have a plan. The Roth will never see us coming. We will do our best to protect Earth, and the Suevans would rather burn all of Roth than lose their mates."

My hands tighten around him. He speaks like it's the truth, and for a moment, it feels like it *is* the truth.

Earth's going to be protected. My crew will be fine. Gen will find her way home to us. The Suevans will get what they want. We're going to be okay.

We're already okay, because we have each other.

His lips graze my forehead in a slow kiss, and then he pulls away from me.

"Ni-Kee," he says, clearing his throat. "I have a surprise for you. I know you did not like the surprise this morning, but I think you will like this one. I hope."

He's so dang cute when he's flustered, his yellow scales on his abdomen flushing with light orange.

I make a show of smoothing my light blue top, pretending to ponder his words.

"Is there food involved with this surprise?"

"I will feed you," he says gravely, his tail twitching.

"Hmmm…. Is there sex involved?" I flutter my eyelashes.

Draz makes a choking sound, his diamond pupils flaring. "Not during the surprise, no. After? As much as your little human body can stand."

"I suppose I can work with that."

He laughs then, the sound pleased and amused. "Come, my heart, let me take you to your surprise. I worked hard on it today."

"Oh, so it wasn't all warlord things?"

"I cannot tell you more, my willful female. It will ruin the surprise if I do."

A flutter of anticipation settles in my stomach, and Draz curls his hand around mine, tugging me out of the myza.

Music floats through the air, and Draz grins at me when I squeeze his hand, looking around for the source of it. Night's begun to settle across the sky, fiery orange streaking the sky, purple playing on the horizon.

He tugs me around the corner, a direction I haven't been yet, and I cover my mouth with my hand. Yellow orbs float around the space—a manicured garden park full of night-blooming flowers. Moon white petals unfurl, spreading a spicy floral aroma that mingles with the unmistakable scent of Suevan cooking.

Tables line the mossy ground, and my crew lets up a cheer when they see me. They seem happy, truly happy, and most have one of the watermelon lime ice drinks in their hands, their loose Suevan clothes painting them in all shades of the rainbow.

There are Suevans here, too, of course, Cephi beams and waves at me from across the way, and a group of burly Suevan warriors cast longing glances at my chattering crew. Their husbands, I realize, and swallow hard.

Draz tucks me into his chest, and I melt into him.

"I thought you would like to relax with your people and mine tonight."

"And not have to fight off giant Crigomar with toxic snails?"

He snorts, tipping a finger under my chin. "I suppose if you truly would like to do that, I can arrange that for your warlord trials."

"I'm sure whatever you normally do will be fine," I laugh, gripping his waist with my hand. He lowers his mouth to mine, and desire winds through me as his lips brush against mine chastely.

"Come, little mate, let us celebrate our union." He leads me into the crowd of Suevans and humans, and the energy is so joyous, so alive, that I want to seize it with both hands and never let go.

It feels like maybe, just maybe, with our two species working together, we can make sense of all our troubles tomorrow.

It feels like hope.

EPILOGUE

One week later

NIKI

TENSION RIDES MY SHOULDERS, pushing them tightly together. My head aches from spending the morning with Tati and Carmen and the Suevan medics, working through the mystery of the translators and acting as a translator myself.

And not a very good one, either.

I groan, trying to work out the kinks in my neck.

"There shouldn't be a problem with them," Tati says, still exasperated. "They should be working."

"Finding out they're not just an implant does shed some light on the situation," Carmen says, rubbing her eyes. "A symbiont." Carmen shoots me a calculating look.

"Why is hers working? It just doesn't make sense," Bex says, walking alongside me, clutching the watermelon lime drink we've all grown quickly addicted to.

"She's our superior officer. Superior in every way," Tati says, and Bex and Carmen laugh.

"What if that is why?" I say slowly. "What if I just… accepted our situation and rolled with it, instead of trying to fight it?"

The laughter dies, and the three of them stare at me as if I've grown another head.

"You mean… you had to consciously accept the symbiont instead of fighting against it?" Carmen taps her fingers against her chin, her mouth screwed up. "I guess it's possible."

"Did you think to yourself, 'I accept my fate, sold like cattle to an alien' and then bam, it worked?" Bex asks, annoyance dripping from every word.

"No, what? No. I don't know… We were just stuck out there, in the jungle, and I realized that my only hope of getting out of there was working with Draz."

"I don't buy it," Bex said, shaking her head. "It's possible, but it doesn't make sense. It's not like the rest of us were crying and beating our chests."

"Not all of you, at least," Tati says glumly.

"I don't know," Carmen says. "It could be that Captain Jacks' neural pathways are more flexible, because of her experience. There might be something to it."

"It can't be as easy as just accepting our situation," Bex snaps. "Otherwise mine would be working."

Carmen and Tati shoot me a look.

"Any word of Gen and her prince?" Tati asks, changing the subject.

My heart sinks. "Not yet."

"We'll find her," Carmen says. "Don't worry about Genevieve. She might seem dainty and delicate—"

Bex snorts. "Yeah, right."

"But she's tougher than all of us. If anyone stands a chance out there, it's Gen and her Suevan."

I chew my bottom lip, worried nonetheless.

"Here comes your alien," Bex says.

Sure enough, Draz strides through the streets toward us,

every inch the brutal warrior. Two other Suevans flank him, and Bex makes an aggravated noise.

"The warlords will escort the humans the rest of the way home," Draz says, and I relay that to them. "You should have waited for us."

We haven't heard many more rumblings from the Suevan separatists, but Draz and I don't want any nasty surprises, so we try to keep the rest of the female humans under constant watch.

Dergoz and Alvez stand tall and proud, and as I watch, Dergoz's jaw twitches as he stares at Bex with open longing.

Huh. I don't really know what's going on between the two of them, but it's not one-sided, that's for sure.

Draz's hands press into my face, and my attention narrows to his breath on my forehead, his heady proximity.

"Hi," I say.

"How did it go?" Draz asks, pulling me back to our myza.

"Not great. We can't figure out why their translators don't work and mine does."

Draz is moving quickly, and I pump my arms, trying to keep up.

"Here, little human," he says, and scoops me up.

"What's the hurry?" I ask, wide-eyed. "Is something wrong?"

His fingers delve into the slit of my skirt, caressing my inner thigh.

"Only that I long to be buried right here, deep inside you."

"Oh, just that? Well, okay then." I huff a laugh that quickly dies, his expert fingers drawing a gasp from me. "Hey, I have something I want to talk about with you."

"Anything," he says, nuzzling my neck and kicking open the door. The zoleh jumps up guiltily, scurrying into the bedroom with one of my boots in her teeth.

We both laugh, sharing a smile, and then his expression turns serious.

"What was it, Ni-Kee?"

"I—" The words fail me, and I swallow hard, trying to work up the courage to tell him what I decided on.

"What is wrong, my heart?" His eyes are wide, his tail slapping the floor behind him.

"Nothing, I just… I think I want to start trying for children. For babies. With you."

His body goes stone still, his eyes wide, and I lick my lips nervously.

"I mean, we don't know how long it might take, right? For me to get pregnant, seeing as how we're different species. But I love you, I love you so much, and I… I've never been so happy. I want to have a family with you."

He lavishes my face and neck with kisses, and I let out a soft moan.

"Ni-Kee, there is no pressure to have babies right now," he says. I squirm as his mouth clamps against one of my nipples, his hands holding me in place.

"But—"

"However, if you are certain, truly certain, then I think we will have much fun practicing."

And he proves to me over and over again how very true that is.

———

For paperback and newsletter exclusive art of Draz and Niki, click here.

Keep reading for a sneak peek of WED TO THE ALIEN PRINCE.

To sign up for my newsletter and be the first to know when the next book comes out, click here.

CHAPTER 42
WED TO THE ALIEN PRINCE SNEAK PEEK

GEN

I'M GONNA FUCKING kill him.

The thought runs through my head, like it has for the last week and a half on this soupy, swamp-ass planet from hell. The alien who's currently number one on my hit list smirks at me, one fang showing in his stupid lopsided grin.

He jabbers something at me, pointing to the snare I've managed to set and spring all in one go.

I can't understand a word he's saying, but I'm pretty damn sure 'I told you so' is written all over his stupidly handsome alien face.

"I didn't do it on purpose," I tell him, crossing my arms. My blonde hair hangs around my face, and I blow at where it tickles my nostrils, trying not to sneeze. "Stop laughing."

He's doing that odd, barking sound, smiling hugely at me now, like this is the funniest thing he's ever seen.

"I don't see you trying to catch dinner, fuckface," I tell him. I called him limp dick a few days ago, but since that seems to be wildly inaccurate for him, I had to stop.

I shouldn't have even noticed anything about his dick, but here we are, in alien jungle purgatory.

He prods the ground with the makeshift spear, using it to hold himself up as he laughs.

"Can you cut me down?" I say, acid in my voice.

He says something else that the translator fails to provide any context for, instead spitting out gobbledygook like 'cupcake head, pretty frosting, understand bacon.'

It gives me a headache. I swing for a moment longer, loathe to ruin the vine-y rope I spent the last three days braiding together to make this snare from. Well, the would-be snare, anyway.

But this asshole doesn't show any inclination to let me down, so I swing harder, before crunching up to untie the knot—

I give a yelp as the alien's talon slices through the vine braid, the awful nightmare sensation of falling triggering near panic. I do not want to break a bone out here. With the high humidity and torrential rains, and God only knows what kind of alien bacteria, any kind of injury could turn deadly.

But strong arms catch me, and I suck in a breath as I look up into his green face.

"Thanks," I say, relieved not to have met the ground.

I wriggle, trying to get free, but he holds me fast.

He points at the vine rope, then down at the ground, shaking his head.

"Yeah, no kidding," I tell him. "I don't want to fall, either."

The alien nods his agreement, saying something else my translator tells me is 'bride fly, not cupcake.' I growl in frustration, and his arms tighten around me.

A primal roar sounds, closer by than it has been the last few nights. My skin prickles, my entire body going into overdrive, screaming that something big and bad is headed our way. The alien crouches, and I try to get free of him, disliking how his over the top alien muscles bunch on top of me. They're huge. It's absurd. I feel tiny next to him, and fragile, and dainty, and I hate it.

I worked hard to be a badass, and he's ruining my self-image.

He tells me something in a low tone, and I grunt in irritation.

'Bad chicken hungry,' the translator unhelpfully provides.

If I could stick my hand in my ear and dig the fucking thing out, I would.

Bad chicken hungry, indeed.

Wed To The Alien Prince on Amazon

ALSO BY JANUARY BELL

ACCIDENTAL ALIEN BRIDES

Wed To The Alien Warlord

Wed To The Alien Prince

FATED BY STARLIGHT

Following Fate: Prequel Novella

Claimed By The Lion: Book One

Stolen By The Scorpio: Book Two

Taurus Untamed: Book Three

NEON RENEGADES

Stranded With The Cyborg: Prequel Novella

Rescued By Her Enemy

Hard Drive

ABOUT THE AUTHOR

January Bell writes steamy sci-fi romance with a guaranteed happily ever after. Combining pure escapism, a little adventure, and a whole lotta love makes for romance that's a world apart. January spends her days writing, herding kids and ducks, and spends the nights staring at the stars.

For the latest updates, follow me on Instagram and Tiktok. Is there a character you would like to see featured in a future novel or novella? Don't be shy! I'd love to hear from you.

Made in the USA
Las Vegas, NV
10 March 2023